WILLOW WITCH

Ghostspeaker Chronicles Book 2

PATTY JANSEN

GET FREE EBOOKS

Visit pattyjansen.com
to sign up for Patty's mailing list. You get four series starter
ebooks for free!

CHAPTER 1

THE BANDITS had been arguing all day.

From the back of her big black horse, Johanna could make out only disjointed parts of their conversation, which was slow and drawn-out, because often the forest was so thick that the twenty or so horses had to ride in single file.

She thought the argument involved directions or orders given to the group by some boss or landowner. A few of the bandits wanted to go to a town, while the main group said that their orders were to go elsewhere, to a place called Hunter's Rest.

None of it meant anything to her. The only town in this area that she was aware of was Florisheim, but she didn't think they were that far upriver yet. Maybe they were in Gelre, maybe still in Estland, she wasn't sure.

The bandits' strong eastern accent didn't help matters. The only one Johanna could hear clearly enough to mostly understand was her "own" bandit. He was a warm presence behind her on the horse and his beard tickled in her neck. His hands were big, with dirty-nailed, hairy fingers that strayed often or "accidentally" grabbed her in places where a man's hand had no business being. He would pull her against him so that she could feel the greasy touch of his leather jerkin and would be enveloped in its stench of smoke and sweat.

His name was Ludo, or something similar, and he had a rough voice and shaggy long hair like the two bears that bounded tirelessly between the horses and around the main group. She figured that he argued in favour of following orders and getting paid, but there seemed to be some sort of disagreement about whose orders were the most lucrative and who was most likely to pay.

Sometimes there was a lull in the argument, when one or two of the arguing parties got frustrated and urged their horses to the other side of the group or to the front, out of earshot of the main group. When that happened, the main group went sullen and broody. In these quiet moments, Ludo said soft words to her under his breath. Things like *flower of beauty*, and *who gets to taste the fruit of a maiden's sin* and other suggestive things. Johanna kept trying to shift forward on the rough saddle just as much as he continued trying to sneak his hands to her chest. *Because I can't allow you to fall* he'd say, even though the horse moved at walking pace and had a steady and even gait.

Then, fortunately, some of the arguing bandits would come back before anything worse happened. The most important of these was a man called Sylvan, who looked like he was both the fiercest and the youngest in the group. He rode alone on a magnificent horse that was strong and tall with a magnificent glossy black mane and long fetlocks. Sylvan was a scrawny fellow, with an ugly scar across his face from an injury that had just missed his mouth, but had pulled one corner of it permanently upwards. His cheeks, forehead and arms bore tattoos of unfamiliar symbols. His hair was done up in plaits, which swung about his head when he tossed it back as an expression of frustration, which he did a lot. Sometimes he would pull his horse's reins so that it would rear on its hind legs, and speed off into the forest. For a horse that size, this came with a frightening thunder of hooves that made the regular horses skitter.

Then he would wait by the side of the forest path for the rest of the party to catch up. Usually both bears and one or two of the hounds went with him. The dogs would bark, and someone in the party, usually the bald leader, whose name appeared to be Sigvald, would yell at them to shut up, and he would hurl sharp comments at Sylvan.

Johanna listened and tried to interpret what the men said, and most importantly, where they were going, but she understood only shards of their dialect. The idea of being taken somewhere unfamiliar for money frightened her. Men who did things for money had a reputation of being ruthless. What if they decided to split up the group of prisoners, or kill the most troublesome and worthless of them?

Since starting out, she had been unable to talk to any of the others, not even during the short breaks when the bandits rested their horses.

The bandit who rode before her shared his horse with Roald. Johanna could see only part of the prince's legs, since the bandit was taller and broader than the prince. Roald had screamed a few times when they were first captured, but had been quiet since. Too quiet, Johanna thought. She worried about what the bandit said to him. A single word might upset him enough to do something unexpected and silly, like screaming uncontrollably or banging his head. Even in Saarland, most folk from outside the towns feared halfwits and didn't want anything to do with them. There were stories about people living their lives locked in tiny rooms, or being branded witches and killed. The bandits had to know that he wasn't normal. It wasn't obvious in his looks, but his behaviour would have informed them soon enough.

Nellie and Loesie were somewhere behind her, but since Loesie couldn't speak, and Nellie seemed to have gone paralysed with fear, Johanna had no idea how far behind. With the creep and his questing hands at her back, she didn't want to look over her shoulder and give him the idea that she was curious about him.

So she listened out for Nellie's voice, but heard nothing except the men's drawl in their rough eastern dialects and the *clop clop clop* of horses' hooves on the ground.

The forest was endless. Johanna could make out no clear path. Sometimes they rode between the massive trunks of beech trees, where it was dark underneath and the ground was covered in dead leaves. The only sunlight that made it down to the forest floor came in thin shafts that penetrated the canopy, or patches of brightness in places where a large tree had fallen. The hazy air made the sunlight show up as brilliant rays of light.

Even animals seemed to have fled this place and its pressing silence. Every breath of wind made leaves rustle. Their lilting and whispering voices formed an eerie background to the arguing from the bandits.

Occasionally they would come to a patch of birch trees that, with their black and white mottled trunks, looked like ghosts. At those places there would be short shrubs on the ground with filaments of spider web between them.

The ground also grew hillier. Sometimes they'd come to the top of a hill and there would be a view between trees, always showing more trees and the occasional patch of bracken. No paths, no sign of habitation.

Yet the bandits seemed to know where they were going. The only thing Johanna could say was *southeast,* judging by the direction of the sunlight.

Their day-long argument dragged on, and with each confrontation came a sharp exchange of words, a moment of Sylvan's posturing where he would pull up his horse so that it stood in the way of the others, and Sigvald would shout at him until he moved. Each time Johanna thought that the two would come to a fight.

If that happened, she guessed each of the bandits would take sides. They would watch the fight and it would be a good time to try to escape. She distracted herself from worrying about Ludo's questing hands by making plans for what she would do. Some of the bags tied to the backs of the five pack-horses looked like they contained tents and blankets. They would have to take those horses.

She didn't know much about horses herself, but Roald could ride, she thought. Nellie could be prodded to do so, but Loesie . . . She had no idea what was going on with Loesie. Coming from a farm, she *should* be able to ride, but Loesie was not well. Even before they were captured, she had barely tried to communicate for days. Johanna had assumed that was because Loesie's task had been to look after the ship, but there had been no warmth or any kind of emotion in Loesie's expression for a long time. Since the burning of Saardam, Johanna thought.

Loesie seemed to have drawn into herself, and Johanna was no longer sure that she listened to what people around her said. If they had the opportunity to escape and had to make a run for it, would Loesie be able to follow simple instructions? What was going on inside her friend's head?

By the time the light turned golden and Sigvald called the party to a halt, there had been no fight and no opportunity to escape.

The horses stopped, blowing gusts of air out of their nostrils, tossing great black-maned heads. Ears twitched and great eyes roved.

Now that the rear of the group caught up with the front, Johanna could see the others. Roald sat as stiff as he had when Johanna had last seen his face. That was just after they had been captured. The bandits had tied his arms, which caused him a lot of distress. He'd been wailing and Johanna had protested to the bandits that he was little danger to anyone, because he was simple. She wasn't sure how much of it the bandits understood, but they had untied his arms and let him ride. The last time she met his eyes, she had told him to sit up in the saddle and be proud. To her surprise he was still following that order, although the rawness in her own backside had caused her to slump ages ago.

It made her feel guilty.

The bandit riding with Loesie had used a rope to lash her to the saddle so she didn't fall off. She sat slumped, her head forward. Johanna thought for a moment that she was asleep, but then she slowly raised her head. Her mouth hung open. Her chin and front of her dress were wet from drool and eyes were unfocused.

Definitely getting worse.

Johanna tried to catch her attention, but she just stared into nothingness. It was as if Loesie had not only lost her voice, but had now also lost the ability to communicate in other ways. She hadn't been like that when Johanna had met her in the markets. It was as if the spell was still eating away at her.

The bandit behind Loesie on the horse was a grizzled, older man with a long and straggly beard and several missing teeth. Johanna met his eyes over Loesie's shoulder. His irises were cloudy white.

Johanna's heart jumped. She hadn't noticed those eyes before. She knew that sometimes older people's eyes went like that, and then they'd see poorly. It was a coincidence, right? She hadn't really affected him with her magic, right?

Your friend is already dead, said a voice inside her head that sounded like Reverend Romulus.

"Johanna, did you even hear what I said?" Nellie's face was scrunched up as if she was about to burst into tears.

"I didn't. I was . . ." *wondering if Loesie's condition is infectious.* "Sorry, what did you say?"

"I said I don't think I can walk anymore, I'm so sore," Nellie said.

"You can walk just fine."

"But it hurts!" Her lip quivered.

"Come on, Nellie," Johanna said under her breath.

She hurt, too. That was what happened if you weren't used to riding, even if the horses only moved at a slow pace. The shifting of weight, trying to stay in the saddle and trying to move away from Ludo had made her backside raw.

Sigvald gave the reins of his horse to another bandit and made his way out of the group. To the right was a slight rise in the beech forest, a broad mound with trees growing at its sides. Sigvald climbed the mossy flank, where exposed tree roots had made uneven natural steps.

He stopped at the top of the hill and peered in all directions. Obviously liking what he saw or didn't see, he gestured for the others to come. Most of the bandits got off their mounts and led their horses by the reins, but Sylvan rode. Ludo rode, too. The horse made small steps so as not to trip over tree roots that had become exposed on the sloping ground.

The little hill had a flat top. The hounds already stood there, making excited squeaking noises and wagging their tails.

From the top of the hill Johanna could see why Sigvald had stopped here. A creek ran through the valley on the other side of the hill, and on the far bank was a little glade with the first grass and meadow plants she had seen since leaving the orchard where they had been captured.

The bandits all dismounted and took off their horses' saddles and packs. One of the younger bandits took two horses down to the glade to graze.

Ludo let himself drop from the saddle and offered to lift Johanna down.

She glared at him. "Keep your hands to yourself, you creep."

He must have gotten the message, because he went to Nellie. Johanna swung her leg over the side of the horse and peeked at the ground and then wished she hadn't looked. Oh boy, it was a long way down. This horse was a giant, much bigger than the coach horses in Saardam. The younger bandit was already coming back up the hill to take the next two horses to the glade. Not wanting anyone else offer her "assistance" dismounting, Johanna let herself slip feet first from the saddle.

She half-fell and landed hard in the leaves. Ouch.

Ludo had convinced Nellie to let him help her. He first supported her legs and then took her by the waist to set her down on the ground.

Johanna was about to warn Nellie, when she exclaimed, "Hey, keep your hands off me!" She yanked herself out of Ludo's grip and took a swipe at him. "What do you think I am, some cheap woman?" Her hand missed Ludo's face.

Most of the bandits had been rolling out sleeping mats and looked around. One or two laughed. Johanna couldn't see the old guy with the cloudy eyes anymore.

Sylvan glared at his companions, his gaze stopping at Ludo. He sat with his ankles crossed, leaning against a tree trunk. He made a sharp comment. Johanna caught something about making a fire before it got dark. Ludo stomped off after muttering something about slaves, either about being a slave or that they had slaves who should do the work instead.

"Oh, Mistress Johanna, I'm so tired," Nellie cried. "You know I work all day and should be used to it, but this . . ." Her voice wavered.

"You don't need to tell me that. I'm tired, too." It was ages since Johanna had ridden a horse and she certainly hadn't done it for very long back then.

Loesie sat on a tree root, her arms looped around her knees. Her eyes had clouded over again.

"I thought it was a nice ride, wasn't it?" Roald said.

"No, it wasn't! We're prisoners and that smelly man behind me kept rasping his throat and spitting. Disgusting."

"Shh, Nellie." Johanna said.

Nellie raged on, "I don't want to be quiet about it. Where are these filthy bandits taking us?"

"Be quiet. Some of them will be able to understand you."

"I don't care." Nellie's voice cracked. "What now? They expect us to sleep on the ground here? With all these men? We can't even understand any of them. All their words sound like *ghghghghgh*." She made a harsh noise in her throat.

Loesie gave a low hiss, but Johanna wasn't sure if it was directed at Nellie.

Calm down, she mouthed at Loesie, but the reaction chilled her. Whatever lived inside Loesie was taking over her mind.

"Hey, you . . . water!" Sigvald yelled. He threw a bucket in Johanna's direction. It was a battered farm bucket, stolen likely.

Johanna couldn't help thinking about the burnt farm where they had found their supplies. The burnt kitchen, the dead bodies. And the *Lady Sara* still waiting for them at the riverside. She hoped the sea cows had enough to eat, or that someone would release them from their harnesses before the animals starved. Then another scary thought: someone might take off with the *Lady Sara,* and it was all she had left from her comfortable life in Saardam. Her father would need the ship if he was to keep running the company.

"Water!" Sigvald repeated with the sharp wave of a hand.

"Yeah, I'm going." Johanna picked up the bucket. "Keep an eye on Loesie," she whispered to Nellie. "And Roald, too."

Nellie nodded, her mouth set in a grim line.

Slowly Johanna picked her way down the side of the hill, between the gnarled tree roots.

Sigvald yelled behind her to hurry up, and added some words that made the other bandits burst out in laughter.

Last thing she heard was Nellie's voice, saying something about, *Do you call that bread?*

The bread the bandits had given their prisoners at midday was heavy, grainy and almost black. Johanna had seen the type before on her trip to Lurezia, where her father's colleagues had shared this type of bread with wine and rich cheeses. On its own, and stale, it had proven a little less easy to swallow.

Now Nellie was asking about beds, speaking loudly and slowly.

Johanna cringed. She had better get the water before Nellie got into too much trouble. She had never expected a demure maid like Nellie to become so doggedly stubborn about their treatment. It was almost frightening.

A carpet of leaves covered the hillside. They were wet and slippery and once Johanna almost lost her footing. This brought forth another burst of laughter from the young man who was walking down another set of horses, without packs or saddles. He splashed through the stream and led his charges up the other bank and into the glade on the far side, where four horses were already grazing.

Upstream from the place where the horses had crossed, the water collected in a clear pond. Small ripples indicated where water creatures swam underneath. The ground was so soft here that her clogs sank in the mud.

Johanna reached as far as she could and splashed the bucket in, but it was too shallow and all she got was a small amount of water and a lot of mud and leaves. Well, stuff that. The glare from the grassy glade across the creek made it hard to see how deep the water was.

Johanna stared at the horses, wishing that she could join them and lie in the grass. No, she wanted to escape from these bandits and that horrible Ludo with his groping hands. Her legs itched to run, but there was no point. She couldn't leave Nellie with that creep. They'd kill Loesie, or Roald, or maybe both. Why had these men kidnapped such an odd group anyway?

Because some of us look like we have money? Roald's fine hands, for example. And Nellie's lace bonnet.

But if the bandits were really interested in money, they would have killed the four of them and taken off with the *Lady Sara*.

Even if she tried to run off alone, she wouldn't get far with all the bandits watching her and the horse boy bringing another two horses to the glade. They knew this forest; she did not. They trusted the forest; she heard voices in the whispering of the wind.

"Water!" Sigvald yelled.

"Yeah, I'm not your slave," she muttered under her breath.

A bit further, a tree branch had fallen across the creek. Maybe she could reach a deeper spot from there. The creek banks were steeper here, so the fallen tree trunk was harder to reach.

But in one spot on the slope stood a small sapling.

Johanna carefully climbed back up the mossy bank and let herself slide down feet first until she caught the sapling. Then she used the trunk of the sapling to lower herself—

As soon as her hand touched the trunk, the forest changed into a scene of chaos and darkness. Men on horses, rearing and screaming. A couple of peasants huddled together. An older man, and a grey-haired grandmother. Children crying in their mother's skirts.

Men with burning sticks.

Slashing swords. A burning house.

The next morning. Blue-grey light of dawn. Trails of smoke over the grass.

So much blood in the creek.

The cloying scent of it enveloped her, and made her feel sick.

With difficulty, Johanna yanked her hand away from the trunk of the sapling. The golden light of the afternoon returned.

Her heart thudded.

These horrible things had happened in this place not so long ago. She peered at the far end of the glade, in the shade of the trees, and now noticed what she hadn't seen before: the glade was not a natural field at all. The creek looped back around the glade. In the shelter of the trees stood the remains of a house. Next to it, a water mill, its magnificent wheel ruined and useless.

The bandits chose to camp here, in a scene of murder and plunder?

If they considered this a safe place for the night, they would have to know who killed the farmer and his family. Maybe they were even the ones who had done it.

And then: why had she seen these things? This was a beech sapling, not a willow tree.

HER LEGS SHAKING, Johanna filled the bucket. She clambered up the steep incline back to the hilltop, avoiding the touch of any more trees. Loud voices and laughter rang through the forest, and the screams of a woman.

No, please. Nellie.

Johanna hurried as much as she could without spilling the water. At the top of the hill the bandits had a fire going. One of the men came to take the bucket off Johanna, but she ignored him.

That sleazy Ludo had grabbed Nellie from behind. She wormed herself away from his free hand that was trying to find a way under her dress.

Johanna didn't think. She swung the bucket so that the water flew out over both Nellie and Ludo. It wasn't a very good throw and most of the water missed, hitting a couple of packs and someone's sleeping mat.

Ludo looked up at her, water dripping from his hair. His large and hairy hand covered Nellie's mouth. Nellie's eyes were so wide that the whites showed on all sides.

"Let her go," Johanna said in as harsh a voice as she could make it.

Ludo laughed and squeezed Nellie's side. He said something about enjoying sweet fruit.

Nellie gave a squeak. A couple of the men guffawed.

"Let her go," came a clear male voice.

Johanna turned around. It was Roald who had spoken. He stood with his back straight and his thumbs in the simple belt that went around the rough knitted farmer's vest that he wore. The orange light from the setting sun cast his face in strong relief. That and his unshaven chin made him look older and more stern than normal. She had told him to behave like a prince a number of times. She imagined that throughout his life, a lot of other people had told him the same. Somewhere, those words must have stuck, because even in farm clothing, he looked so much like his father it was eerie.

He's the king now. We must have a crowning ceremony when we get to a safe place. She thought of the staff and crown which she had hidden in the broom cupboard.

Roald said, "Let her go, brute. These are my women."

Oh, by the heavens.

"That be so?" Ludo said "Two women for one man, huh?" He continued with a remark of sexual nature that Johanna didn't need to understand word for word to get the gist of it.

The other bandits laughed and jeered at Roald. He took no notice of them, but took Nellie's arm and pulled.

"Watch what I do to *your* women." Ludo's hand found the buttons at the front of Nellie's dress and started to undo them, revealing Nellie's white underdress like a peeled fruit.

Nellie wriggled and kicked.

"Let her go!" Roald took Ludo's arm with both hands and tried to yank him off Nellie, but he was so much smaller and skinnier than the bandit that Ludo dragged both Nellie and

Roald around as if neither weighed anything, while Roald struggled to maintain his footing and Nellie desperately tried to do her buttons back up.

Several of the younger bandits were laughing so hard that the tears ran over their cheeks.

Not Sylvan. He still leaned against a tree trunk, his legs crossed at the ankles. The intense look in his brown eyes made Johanna shiver.

A magician?

The two bears lay on the ground next to him, leaning their shaggy heads on their paws. Nothing moved about them except their eyes.

Sigvald wasn't laughing either. He stood on the far side of the fire, watching the struggle with his arms crossed tightly over his chest.

Just as Roald had gotten his feet under him, one of the younger bandits tripped him up from behind.

Then Sylvan pushed himself off the tree trunk. In one fluid motion, he jumped to his feet, rising well over both Ludo and Roald's heads. He wore very dark clothing, and although he was not broad like some of the others, his height made him imposing. The scar on his face even more so.

Ludo stopped dragging Nellie around.

Sylvan brushed Roald aside as if he was a fly. He grabbed the front of Ludo's jerkin, ignoring the presence of Nellie between them.

Everyone fell quiet.

"You are so much interested in selling them, right?" His speech sounded a lot more sophisticated than that of the others.

Ludo retreated ever so slightly.

"Who do you think will pay for damaged goods?"

Ludo made a protest about *just having some fun.*

Sylvan retorted with a harsh remark in dialect that sounded like it meant, "Stop behaving like a child."

Ludo growled, "Oh, fuck off." And added something about bashing his face in and being a soft boy.

"I dare you to try." Sylvan let go of Ludo's jerkin. He yanked Nellie out of Ludo's grip. She squeaked, but he roughly pushed her aside, as if clearing the scene for a fight. Nellie tripped with the force of his push, and fell into the leaf litter.

Johanna rushed to help her up.

"Oh, Mistress Johanna!" Nellie cried. Her face was white, with the imprint of Ludo's hand still over her mouth. She closed Nellie in her arms. Nellie trembled.

Poor Nellie.

Father had appointed Nellie soon after her mother had died, to be a companion to Johanna as a girl. Nellie had been fourteen when she joined the household, and was in many ways, more than Johanna's governess. Nellie might be silly and annoying at times, but she was the closest thing Johanna had to a sister.

Sylvan and Ludo circled one another, under the bandits' cheering.

Over Nellie's shoulder, Johanna scanned the forest for an avenue of escape. She'd planned to use a fight as a time to escape, but now that it happened, it was not a good time to try anything. Most of the horses were now in the glade, and would probably be hard to catch and even harder to ride without reins, and she wasn't that confident that she could put them on quickly. The packs had all been taken down from the horses and there would be no time to sort out what they needed. If they ran now, they could only do so without supplies, and who knew how far the nearest town was?

The two bears had risen and stood behind Sylvan. One of the animals emitted a low growl.

Ludo charged. Sylvan simply stepped out of his way. Ludo swung his fist, but Sylvan ducked. He brought his fist up from underneath. The hand connected with Ludo's jaw with a clearly audible thud. Ludo cried out, and stopped Sylvan punching again by holding him in a strong hug.

They two men pushed against each other. Sylvan tried to free himself but, not being strong enough, only succeeded in pushing the pair of them around in a resemblance of some strange dance.

The other bandits gathered, laughing and shouting. Finally, Sylvan managed to free himself from Ludo's grip. Ludo tried a few punches, but Sylvan was too quick and easily avoided them. Ludo charged and caught Sylvan around the middle. The two toppled onto the leaf-covered ground. At that moment, one of the bears jumped on top of Ludo's back. It grabbed hold of Ludo's jerkin and pulled, ripping a hole in the leather. Then it grabbed Ludo's hair and pulled his head back. Ludo's eyes went wide, showing whites on all sides.

Nellie gave a squeal. "Oh, it's going to kill him!"

But then Sylvan whistled, and the animal let go of Ludo's hair.

Ludo rubbed the back of his head, covered in bear slobber. He pushed himself up to his knees while glaring at Sylvan and breathing heavily.

Then he started laughing. Sylvan laughed, too, albeit a bit more stiffly, and all the bandits joined in, clapping each other on the shoulders. The two bears dropped back in their sleeping position into the leaf litter.

Johanna joined Roald, Nellie and Loesie at the base of a large tree a little away from the fire.

Nellie whispered to her, "Thank you helping me. I was so afraid that they were going to harm me."

"Shh, Nellie, it's all right. Of course we would help you."

"But they're so big and we're all so small. I'm scared. That man is such a piece of filth."

"Tell me about it. I've sat on the horse with him all day."

"Oh, Mistress Johanna, you shouldn't have to go through that. You're married."

"Not like he cares about that. Listen, we don't need to be big, we need to be smart. The first chance we get, we're going to escape and get back to the *Lady Sara*." But deep inside she was scared, too. Next time, the outcome of a confrontation like this might not be as good. If Ludo got it in his mind that he wanted to do indecent things to either her, Nellie or Loesie, there would be nothing to stop him.

Nellie asked, "Do you think you could still find your way back to the river?"

"I think so." But in reality? She thought she knew the direction the river would be if it were a straight line. But rivers were rarely straight lines, and they had been riding through this forest for hours. All trees looked the same. If they escaped, how could they get back? With dogs and horses, the bandits would capture them again soon.

She shrugged but avoided Nellie's eyes. To flee successfully, there had to be a place to flee to.

The bandits got serious about producing something to eat. One of the younger bandits had caught two rabbits which Johanna had seen dangling at the back of his saddle earlier in the day. Another man brought a larger animal, with a shorthaired brown coat, a long neck and long graceful legs. Sigvald sent two young men off to skin the animals.

"It's a deer," Roald said.

Johanna had heard of deer, but had never seen any. "Do they all have horns like that?"

"They're called antlers. This one is a young male. Older males have bigger antlers."

Sylvan gave him a suspicious sideways glance as if he wanted to say *What do you know about it?*

"They're good eating," Roald continued.

"Who says you get any?" Sylvan's voice was harsh and strongly accented. Each time he met her eyes, Johanna felt a chill going through her.

Slowly, he rose and strolled to the spot where they sat.

Magic was in everything he did: from the way he sniffed the air to the way he whistled at the bears and the way they obeyed him without the need for chains and cages. It was in the way he argued with the others and the way he rode off on his big horse. Danger swirled about him like a cloak.

He faced the prisoners and sank into a crouch, resting his elbows on his bent knees, studying each of them in turn.

Nellie cowered under his gaze. He simply laughed at her in a way that said *I'm not even interested enough in you to do you any harm.*

Roald stared back at him, and Sylvan held his gaze for such a long time that Johanna felt chilled. There were rumours of people who could read minds, but those rumours were all lies, weren't they?

Sylvan shifted his gaze to her. His brown eyes narrowed, but he remained quiet for a long time. Then he said, "Interesting."

What he found interesting he neglected to mention.

Then he turned to Loesie. He bent closer, looking her in the eyes. "You're magic-touched, eh?"

She kept staring as if he had said nothing.

He pushed her shoulder.

Loesie flew up, making a low hissing sound. Her eyes had gone white again. Johanna shivered with the chill of magic that went through her.

Sylvan laughed. "You're a little cat, eh?" Didn't he feel it?

"Leave her alone," Roald said.

"She belongs to you, too? *Your* women? What do you think you are?"

"I'm—"

"Shhh," Johanna said, before Roald could give away anything.

Sylvan looked from Roald to her and back again, but said nothing.

He poked Loesie again, and she tried to scratch him, but he yanked his hand back quickly.

She growled.

Another bandit got up. "Let me try." He poked her. He wasn't quite so quick in retreating and received a nasty scratch to his arm.

Sylvan laughed. "Now your blood's poisoned and you become a witch, too."

The man's eyes widened. "What? Yer kidding, right?"

The other bandits burst into laughter.

Sigvald didn't laugh. He stood on the other side of the fire and watched, unemotional, with his arms crossed over his chest. The firelight glinted on his bald head.

His eyes met Johanna's. They were cold, calculating. She feared that he knew exactly who she and Roald were. If he came regularly to the towns on the Rede River, he might know the *Lady Sara* or the Brouwer Company flag. He would certainly recognise the marks of the Saarlander royal family, and if not . . . the bandits only needed to search their prisoners, and they would find the ring on the chain around Johanna's neck, and they would find the Carmine crest on Roald's underclothes.

Roald said, "I was only going to protect you from that man. You don't want me to say anything?"

"Don't say anything if it isn't necessary."

"I was only trying to answer the brute's questions."

"They are not our friends. We don't answer questions."

"But Mother says it's polite to—"

"We don't need to be polite. They took us against our will."

Johanna didn't know if Roald understood, or even remembered how they'd been captured, but at least he shut up. Fancy not understanding the concept of being a *prisoner*.

And then another, more chilling, thought: *He's been a prisoner all his life*, like a bird in a gilded cage. People would have been telling him what to do, and most likely he never wanted to do any of those things. Come to a tea party at the palace? Hold a speech? Dance with a string of nervous girls? Get on this boat? Look after these horses? He might not even understand that there had been a difference in his freedom.

Sylvan went back to the fire with a toss of his head.

The young men had returned with the skinned rabbits and the deer and hung them over the fire. One of them sat down at the fire, turning the spit.

Sigvald pulled out a flask which he unstoppered and drank a good swig. He passed it to Ludo, who drank, too, and wiped his mouth.

Soon, the men were all talking and drinking.

Johanna remained with Nellie, Roald and Loesie at the base of the big tree. It was getting cold this far from the fire. Nellie was shivering, but neither Loesie nor Roald seemed to be bothered by the chill.

The bandits talked and laughed. Occasionally the waft of the smoke and the increasingly wonderful smell of the meat drifted in their direction.

"I'm hungry," Roald said.

"We're all hungry." Johanna met Sigvald's eyes again across the orange glow of the fire as he lifted the bottle to his mouth and drank.

"I don't like these monks," Roald said.

"These are not monks." If they were, they'd have some dignity and manners.

"I don't care, I don't like them anyway. They're rude."

Johanna whispered, "Shh, not so loud."

The old grizzled fellow who had shared his horse with Loesie was telling a story. Johanna caught shards of information about a beautiful widow with a young daughter who had rejected his advances. Several of the men made snide remarks about the old fellow's missing teeth and his attractiveness to women.

"What dialect do they speak to each other?" Nellie asked.

"It's Eastern Burovian," Roald said.

Johanna frowned at him. "But we're not in Burovia." As far as she guessed, they were in Gelre. Burovia was on the other side of the Rede River. "Can you understand them?"

"A bit. The monks all speak the same."

Nellie started, "They're not—"

"Leave it, Nellie."

Sylvan got up from the fire and came to them, carrying a leg of meat, dripping fat. He placed it on a wooden plank and proceeded to cut chunks of meat off it with a knife so sharp that he hardly had to make any effort to slice through the meat. One of his bears sat on its haunches behind him, observing his actions with black beady eyes. Waiting to be tossed scraps.

"Eat," he said.

Behind him, at the fire, the bandits broke into loud raucous laughter. Most had red faces from the liquor, but she hadn't spotted Sylvan drink anything.

Johanna took a slice of the meat from the plank he held out to her. "Where are you taking us?"

"You would like to know, huh?"

"Well, yes. I don't understand what you want from us. We're only three innocent women and a harmless man."

"Why were you travelling with a witch with magic so strong that I can feel her presence from miles off?"

Loesie?

Johanna glanced at her friend, who was stuffing pieces of meat in her mouth with both hands. She chewed open-mouthed, letting a trail of fat run down her chin. Johanna remembered the incident with the cheese. A chill went down her spine. She had trusted Loesie with the sea cows, and Loesie had taken the *Lady Sara* upstream as Johanna had told her. She had trusted Loesie not to betray them. "She is not a witch. She has been affected by magic, that is true."

But what if she was wrong, and it was all part of an evil plan and Loesie had been ordered to take the ship upstream by the person who had put the spell on her?

He said, "Witch or bewitched, all the same thing."

No, it wasn't, and if he knew anything about magic, he would know that. More likely, he was lying. "So why do you want her?"

"We protect land from evil magic."

Then why do I feel magic about you? The look on his face was dead-serious. What did people here believe about magic? As far as she knew, the eastern Belaman Church also forbade it. The Church of the Triune was considered a splinter group of the Belaman Church, and had more in common with it than either side acknowledged.

"What are you going to do with us?"

"The Duke will decide. Now eat. We have no use for dead witches." He put the board down and watched while Roald put a piece of meat in his mouth. Then he rose and turned back to the fire.

"He scares me," Nellie said when he had taken his place with the other bandits again.

Johanna nodded. Nellie might not have any magic, but she

had a good sense of trust. "I don't know who he is, but he's not one of the regular bandits."

"Do you know what all those tattoos mean?"

"I think they're old runes. I went through Burovia with Father once, and we saw old shrines along the river with marks like that. Can't say if they were exactly the same, though." She looked aside when Sylvan turned his head in her direction, as if he knew they were talking about him. The firelight made the scar across his cheek deeper and uglier than it looked in daylight.

"How dare he call us witches?" Roald said, his mouth full.

"He's talking nonsense," Johanna said.

"Yes, we're not witches. I will teach these monks that they can't say things like this." He made to get up.

"Sit down, please," Johanna said. "We need to plan this."

To her surprise, he listened.

"We need to make a plan to get away," Johanna continued in a low voice. "But we need to be smart about it so that the bears can't smell us." The creatures in question were looking at her with their black beady eyes.

"I think we should wait until we come to a town," Nellie said. "You often say things because you like to believe that they're true, but I don't believe you can find your way back to the *Lady Sara*."

"We'll find our way, once we escape. It might not be the shortest way, but we'll get there."

Nellie pursed her lips.

No one said anything for a while.

"Who is this Duke?" Nellie asked a bit later.

"I have no idea," Johanna said.

"I think we are close to Duke Lothar's land," Roald said.

Johanna frowned at him. She had to keep reminding herself that he'd spent the past few years in this region. "Who is he?"

"Duke Lothar Anselmus Wilhelmus de Marty-Loessinger, duke of Nieheim, prince of Florisheim, commander of—"

"We don't need the entire page of names."

"He considers himself second in line to the Barony of Gelre. He is Baron Uti's half-brother, older than him, but born of the wrong blood. The Baroness Machteld, who is Uti's mother, gave birth to only one son. Lothar is the son of the Baroness' sister Gunhilde, who was much prettier than Machteld and whose four children are said to have had four different fathers, one of which was Uti's father."

Nellie frowned at him. "That's a lot of terrible gossip about a single royal family. It's not very nice."

"It's true. Things that are true don't need to be nice."

"Who told you all this?" Johanna asked.

"Everyone knows this. Especially about Gunhilde. The duke doesn't look like the Baroness Machteld at all."

Everyone in Burovia where he had been maybe, but it was news to Johanna. "But the baron does not consider the duke in line to the throne?"

"No, but the duke thinks he should be. He tried to kill his half-brother twice. Last time was two years ago, when he hosted a dinner for the baron and his family in his castle and planned to poison them. When the baron found out, a lot of the duke's people were cast out of Florisheim."

"I bet they were." They'd probably gone on to become rogues. Maybe these bandits were some of them.

"Why would the duke be interested in us?" Nellie asked.

Roald didn't answer that question. It was probably beyond him. He knew facts and he knew how to do things by routine, but he had trouble doing something with those facts and drawing conclusions from them.

Johanna thought she knew why the duke was interested in them: because of magic. And she wondered how much this had to do with Roald's stay in Burovia and a certain religious

order, or with Baron Uti's presence at the ball, and maybe—
she shuddered—maybe the burning of Saardam was simply
another attack on Baron Uti, dressed up as an invasion by
rogues. Had he died in the fire, too?

Some pieces of the puzzle were coming together.

The main figure in the war was Baron Uti, whose son had
told Johanna that Gelre used magic at court. And here were a
bunch of rogues who wanted to protect the land from magic,
or maybe just any magic that was not the right kind, and they
worked for the duke.

And the conflict was also about a Burovian religious order,
and religious groups forbade magic. And about a king who
was said to have been in negotiation with a necromancer,
necromancy being a serious form of black magic.

Wasn't this starting to sound like the Church of the
Triune had a hand in it? That same church that had been
banned from most lands?

Johanna ate her chunks of meat, which were dry, over-
cooked and hard to chew.

Nellie was having trouble as well. "This meat is very
stringy." She wriggled her tongue in her mouth as illustration

"It's because it's a deer," Roald said. "They live in the
forest and have to be tough. There's deer, and wild pigs, and
badgers, but they're not very good eating. Pheasants and
rabbits are, but they live near fields."

"Have you seen all these things?"

"Seen them, caught them, eaten them. Pheasants are best,
but you have to pluck all their feathers and that's annoying."

Nellie said, "I don't know how you could stand it, with all
these horrible oak trees."

"Beech, not oak. Beech trees are nice and tidy. Oak trees
have big knots."

"Well, whatever." Her voice sounded angry, close to
breaking.

"No, it's important. With oak trees, you can—"

"I don't care! I hate this forest! It's disgusting! I am disgusting, and there is nowhere to wash anything." She burst into tears.

Johanna put an arm over her shoulder. "Come on, Nellie, I need you to keep it together."

"I'm done with keeping it together. I want clean clothes. Look at this bonnet." She yanked it off. Underneath, her hair was lank and stringy. She lifted up her skirt and showed the underskirt beneath. "Look at my underclothes."

Johanna could smell it before Nellie showed her: the white chemise was streaked through with dark brown stripes of blood. The same dark stripes also ran down the pale skin of the part of Nellie's leg that Johanna could see.

Johanna met Nellie's eyes, pools of embarrassment and horror. "You have your monthly bleeding? Why didn't you say anything?"

"With that disgusting man at my back? He would just have laughed. Ladies' problems are not real problems at all." She buried her face in her hands. "I feel so dirty, Mistress Johanna."

"Cowpats, Nellie. I'm sure we can do something to help you out." She rose and wormed her underskirt from under her dress. She gave Nellie the wad of fabric and noticed that it was pretty dirty, too. "Here. Use this. Wrap it around yourself. Wash it out in the creek tomorrow."

"But it's your best—"

"Use it, Nellie."

Nellie took it without a further word, and went behind the tree.

CHAPTER 3

THE BANDITS talked and drank well into the night. They reduced the deer and rabbits to a pile of bones which they threw to the dogs. The bears got some uncooked chunks of meat, the front legs and the head and neck of the deer, and proceeded to tear strips of meat and sinew off the bones with their teeth. One of the animals then trotted off to the creek and made a mess of the pool where Johanna had tried to collect water. It stood in the shallow water and dug in the sand with its claws. Then it repeatedly stuck its head in the water and nosed around. What it found there to eat, Johanna couldn't see, but it chewed noisily and wetly.

When it got darker, Sigvald made one of the junior bandits get up to pass the prisoners mats and blankets. They were a collection of horse blankets and quilts, probably stolen from farms the group had raided. Johanna noticed that the young man was unsteady on his feet from the liquor. If they escaped now, how many of these men would be too drunk to ride?

The mats were thin. The forest floor was not very

comfortable. The beech trees had knotted roots which came right through the thin mats. The blankets were scratchy and not particularly warm. A musty, unwashed smell hung about them.

Johanna wrapped a blanket around her shoulders, and watched the bandits in the glow of the firelight. Nellie sat to the right of her, her knees drawn up to her chest and her skirt wrapped around her ankles. Roald sat to her left. He didn't seem to be bothered by the chilly night air.

Loesie lay on her side on the mat, facing away from the group. Johanna hoped that she was finally asleep.

The bandits talked and laughed, emptying one flask of liquor after another. Their voices increased in raucousness and their slurred speech made it even more impossible to understand the men. She wasn't sure if any of them understood each other anymore. The old grizzled fellow fell flat on his face when he reached for the bottle. A moment later he was snoring, to the great hilarity of the others.

Johanna dozed a bit, leaning her head on her knees, but she kept falling over, and when she lay down, the ground was too hard to be comfortable. It got cold.

An eerie wailing birdcall echoed in the forest.

Slowly, the fire died to a faint orange glow. There were only three bandits left around it, and one disappeared on the other side of the hill and didn't come back. Another fell asleep, and the last one stumbled to his feet. He stood there swaying, silhouetted against the dying fire, before lumbering off to his mat. Not much later, the men were finally all asleep. A couple of them snored loudly.

The bears also snored, a low rumble.

Johanna dozed off, but jerked awake when that bird called again. She had no idea how long she had been asleep—she guessed not more than a few moments—but her heart was thudding. There were no sounds other than the roaring of blood in her ears.

"Nellie?" Johanna whispered as quietly as she could.

Nothing.

Johanna held her breath to listen, but all she could hear was the bandits' continued snoring.

If they wanted to escape, this was the time to do it, now that the men were all blind drunk and asleep. The bandits had even been drunk enough to forget to tie their prisoners up, or to forget to take the dogs back from the meadow. Johanna nudged at Nellie's shoulder. "Let's go."

"What? Now? By ourselves?" Her voice sounded scared.

"This is our best chance. They're all drunk. The bears are asleep."

"I agree. I don't like these monks at all. We should go," Roald said.

"Shhhh. We don't want to wake them up, especially the animals." She didn't *think* Sylvan would set the bears on them, because obviously they had more value alive than dead, but those dogs down near the creek could make a lot of noise if they were spooked, and wake everyone up.

The meadow was invisible from here. Moonlight made light patches on the canopy, but no moonlight pierced through to the forest floor, where it was dark as ink.

All of a sudden Johanna had to think of what happened last night in the cabin of the *Lady Sara* and how scared and unhappy she had been.

She'd been stupid. They had been safe aboard the *Lady Sara*. In fact, she'd been stupid about getting married for most of her life. She'd been a constant worry for her father, her stubbornness a source of irritation for him, and look where it had got her.

I swear when I get out of this alive, I'm going to be a good wife and make my husband happy every night. She didn't care, she would give anything to be back in that cabin and submit to him again. The only part of her that had been hurt was her pride, and in the scheme of things, she was struck by how utterly unimportant that was.

She crawled to her feet. "Let's go. Take these blankets."

Fumbling in the dark, she rolled hers up, and there were noises that indicated that the others were doing the same.

"Do you really think this is a good idea?" Nellie asked.

"Shhh. Loesie?"

"Does she have to come?" Nellie whispered. "We can come back for them later. She'll attract any people looking for magic."

"Loesie is my friend." Why was Nellie always so annoying? *Because she's usually right.* "Come on, Loesie."

"Hmmmm."

"Can you help her, Nellie?"

"Me? But I can't—"

"Please. Nellie, can you just once do as I say?"

"I always do as you say, Mistress Johanna, and it gets me into a lot of trouble. I don't think this is a good idea."

Please, Nellie, this is not the time to have stupid arguments. But Nellie *was* right. Loesie's presence *would* attract attention. From what she gathered, it was what had attracted the bandits to them in the first place.

"Well, tough," Johanna said to herself. She remembered first meeting Loesie in the markets and feeling the magical connection straight away. Loesie had smiled at her in a mischievous way and had handed her a basket that showed a bull doing unspeakable things to a cow in a wide green meadow. Johanna had laughed, and had asked if the calves were good this year, and then Loesie laughed. The secret of magic that they both shared had become a point of friendship straight away.

Like Johanna, Loesie refused to become what people told her to be.

No matter what the Reverend Romulus had said, Johanna believed that the real, happy, mischievous Loesie was still in that ghostly body somewhere and could be cured if they found the right person.

Leaves rustled nearby.

"I'm ready," Roald whispered. He sounded like a young kid going on an exciting trip.

They started down the hill, feeling their way down the uneven ground. Johanna could only hear the rustling of leaves, and had no idea if Loesie was with them. She hoped so, because she was going to have serious words with Nellie if she kept behaving towards Loesie like this.

They stopped when the ground evened out. Johanna listened for sounds indicating that the bandits or any of the animals had woken up, but could hear none.

It was so dark here that it was impossible to see the slightest thing.

"Which way now?" Roald asked.

"We need to get to the horses."

"Which way is that?"

Johanna studied the forest, most of it in ink-darkness. A faint patch of light indicated where the glade probably was. But she could see no horses. More worryingly, she couldn't see the creek.

"I think this is stupid," Nellie said. A sniff indicated that she was crying. "I don't know if you have seen it, Mistress Johanna, but all these people have magic. If we take the witch, these men will know where she is. Maybe she even attracted them to us in the first place. I'm not being unkind to her, but we can't escape like this. You know how magic seeks out magic? It happens with you and Master Willems and the witch."

"Loesie. Use her name."

"I don't care! They will know where we are because of her."

"Ghghghghghgh!"

"Shhh!" Loesie sounded angry now, and Johanna did *not* want to get Loesie angry because who knew what trouble that would cause.

Nellie whispered as loudly as one could whisper, "There is no point escaping! They will catch us. We don't know where to run. We don't know how to get food when we get lost. We can't—"

"Nellie, what's gotten into you? If we stay, it will end up badly, especially for you. Those men haven't seen a woman for a long time. I might have protected you so far, but there is going to be a time that the creep Ludo drags you behind a bush and we will be too late."

Nellie sniffed. Her breath shuddered. "Just so you know, Mistress Johanna, if I had the choice I'd rather unwillingly lose my virtue to a disgusting hairy brute than die by the hand of ghosts or other vile magic. And that's the truth. Call me a coward if you want."

Johanna had nothing to say to that. Coming from Nellie, this statement was so astonishing that words would be inappropriate. Nellie, whose first life rule was "virtue", followed close behind by "appropriateness". She'd actually said that she'd rather—?

"Hang on, Nellie. What are you so afraid of?"

"There's *things* in that forest. Magical things." Her voice cracked. "Ghosts, wraiths, ghouls. Evil things. It makes me feel ill just thinking about them. This is godless country, and no amount of prayer is going to help us. If we go out there, we *will* get lost and those magical beings will find us. We have no defence. Please, Mistress Johanna." She grabbed Johanna's arm in a surprisingly strong grip.

"Then what do you want us to do?"

"Wait until we come to a town."

"They probably won't take us to a town."

"I don't care. Please don't make me go into that forest. Please." She burst into tears.

Well, great. What now?

"Weren't we going somewhere?" Roald asked.

At the same time Nellie said, "No."

Johanna said, "Yes."

Loesie said, "Ghghghghgh!" The tone of distress in her voice made Johanna turn around.

A *horse* had appeared in the forest. Well, it wasn't a regular horse, but one made from luminous mist, floating a forearm's length above the ground. It walked steadily, trailing tendrils of white vapour.

"Mistress Johanna!" Nellie grabbed Johanna's arm and hid behind her.

Roald said, "How does it do that?" In a genuinely interested voice.

Oh, for the inability to feel fear.

"Ghghghghgh!" Loesie charged forward. With both arms, she mowed into the shining apparition. Shards of mist scattered through the night. They swirled, they re-formed, they grew. One horse became six horses.

They were all quite close, a few paces away, in a half-circle surrounding the group.

"Nooo," Nellie groaned.

"Hmmmm!" Loesie made for the closest horse, her arms raised.

"Stop it, Loesie." Johanna grabbed the back of Loesie's dress. Nellie had sounded like she was about to faint, and she didn't want to have to deal with that, too.

The phantom horses paid the group no attention. They stood with their ears pricked and heads in the air. Nostrils and eyes were wide. They bunched together, as if using each other to seek protection against something, real or ghostly.

Johanna noticed what she hadn't seen before: several of the animals had cuts in their coats. Blood—or its white misty substitute—ran from the wounds. Then a ghostly man ran onto the scene, brandishing a sword. The first animal—a stallion—reared and let out a scream.

In the real forest, the horses in the glade responded with whinnies and snorts. A dog started barking and the other dog joined, growling like crazy.

Men shouted in the forest. Someone came running down the hill carrying a flaming torch.

"Come here, everyone, hide." This was Roald's voice.

Johanna stumbled to where he hid, pressed against the trunk of a large tree. When he held a protective arm around her shoulders, her hand touched the tree's bark.

The forest dissolved for a scene of fire and death. Men on horses burst into a farm yard, carrying torches and rampaging through a vegetable garden. The barn door was open and horses ran out, showing the white in their eyes. Billowing smoke rose from the roof. A woman ran away from the burning house, carrying a child. She was mown down from behind by a rider with a huge sword. The child, a toddler, fell in the mud. The rider hacked at it until it was nothing but a chunk of bloody pulp.

Johanna jerked back from the tree, her heart thudding.

Leaves rustled not far from where they stood, followed by the heavy footsteps and hot breaths of a very large animal. One of the bears. Johanna couldn't see it but it sounded like very close.

"Ghghghgh!" Came from somewhere in the dark.

"Shh, Loesie." Who knew what that bear would do if it became interested in them.

The ghost horses pranced between the trees, being light-footed and luminous, while a couple of the bandits tried to round up the real horses on the meadow. Two bandits with torches stood by the side of the creek. Were they looking for the prisoners? The hounds ran through the forest, panicked, whining, barking at everything. One of them would stop near the bandits with the torch, jump around in a little circle as if chasing its own tail, and then continue running.

Johanna could now see, silhouetted against the glow of torchlight, the fuzzy outline of a bear, much too close. It lifted its head, snorting. Its nose wriggled.

Also silhouetted against the light stood Loesie, with her hand outstretched towards the bear. "Ghghghghghgh."

Johanna held her breath. Any moment now and the bear would pounce and they would all be dead. That was why bandits didn't need to tie up their prisoners: because the bears killed any that tried to escape.

Loesie didn't move.

Johanna sat as frozen. She didn't want to see what happened but couldn't tear her eyes away from that silhouette: Loesie with her hand outstretched, the bear lifting its head to her . . . sniffing her palm.

For several long moments, nothing happened. The blood roared in Johanna's ears. Then the animal grunted, lowered its head and trudged back up the hill. A wisp of magic trailed behind it. Loesie said nothing but Johanna could feel the magic in the air. Bear magic, which was said to be evil.

Where did Loesie learn these things? As far as Johanna knew, Loesie only had willow magic, like her.

In her mind, she heard the Shepherd's voice. *Likely, your friend is already dead and demons have possessed her body.*

Way back when all this started, Loesie *did* try to warn her about demons, right? Johanna thought back to that horrible moment when she had seen Loesie at her market stand and realised there was something very wrong with her friend.

Inside her mind, the Shepherd's voice said, *They show us what we like to see.*

What did she like to see? Loesie still in control of her mind, even though she couldn't speak. Loesie recovering. Loesie being the normal, happy Loesie, and speaking again, being healthy again.

A couple of the bandits were now coming back up the hill with one of the dogs. Johanna didn't think the bandits knew the prisoners had gone, but there was no escaping now. There were no places to hide in this forest, and both the hounds and bears would find them quickly, even if they tried to run.

"Let's go back," she said. And hope that the bandits wouldn't notice.

Slowly, they walked back up the hill. The further they progressed, the angrier she became with herself. She had hesitated too much when it mattered. Since when was she afraid of the things she saw in wood? Since when had she been such a coward?

Since seeing that awful forest in Burovia, and hearing its whispering voices.

They found the hilltop abandoned except for a single bear, and resettled at the tree with their blankets. The bear lifted its head, sniffed the air, grunted and put its head back down on its paws.

Johanna pulled the blanket over herself and leaned into Roald, who awkwardly put an arm around her shoulders. His breath tickled her hair.

For a long time, none of them said anything. The bandits were still walking around the forest, coming up the hill to relight their torches in the fire, and shouting to each other. Something about a missing horse and people being out there to steal horses. The latter was Sigvald's concern.

But no thieves were found and after a while, the missing horse turned up as well and all the men came back. They returned to their mats, still talking to each other in the glow of the fire. Their voices were angry. Johanna thought she heard Sylvan's voice most of all. He sat on the other side of the fire and seemed to be angry over someone going somewhere or allowing the horses or dogs to come to a place *where the dead live* whatever that might mean. But after a while the argument faded into brooding periods of silence. Eventually the participants went back to sleep.

"We sleep now?" Roald asked.

"Yes." Then she added, her voice low, "Thank you for standing up for Nellie earlier tonight. I thought that was very brave of you. I'm sorry that they teased you."

"No one can touch my women."

She didn't like being referred to as anyone's possession, but she was glad that he considered Nellie part of the deal. She wondered if the feeling stretched to Loesie, but didn't want to push the point. "Be careful, though. These are dangerous men. Some of them are magicians."

"I'm not afraid of them."

No, she feared as much. She suspected he couldn't lie. Maybe he didn't have the capability for fear either. Right now, she felt jealous of his simplistic way of thinking. He didn't worry much; he just lived. He knew lots of things, but attached little emotional value to them or even to his life. When someone said, "Walk," he walked. He protected what he considered his property.

In the space under the blanket, his body was warm against hers, and in an odd way, comforting. She *needed* that, because she was running out of ideas and no one else seemed to have any.

"I'm sorry," he said.

"What for?"

"I can't look at you tonight. It's not that I don't want to see you, but it's too dark here. I can't see anything."

Johanna almost laughed. "That's all right. You can look some other day." After all the things that had happened, that was what he thought about?

"Yes. I want that. It's good."

If ever they were safe and warm enough, if she could convince him to be gentler, if they were in a comfortable and clean bed, it might be good. Or even in the too-narrow and not so very clean bunk in the *Lady Sara*'s cabin. The thought of the ship left abandoned at a disused jetty on the river made her eyes prick. That was part of her family's wealth, back there. She owed it to her father to try to get back to the ship. And the thought of her father brought more tears.

Roald said, "I just remembered something. My mother said that when I married, I had to tell my wife at least once every day that I loved her. I haven't done that yet. Do you want me to say it three times to make up for it?"

Johanna choked up. For a long time she couldn't speak, trying to swallow away tears which came anyway, leaked out of her eyes and ran over her cheeks. Eventually she managed to control her voice just enough to say, "Just once will be enough. It doesn't become different or better by repeating it."

"It does. Every day, she said, because it's one of the things that people forget to say to each other."

"Oh, you silly." She pressed herself against him, wanting to snuggle in his arms, but likely he didn't even understand the importance of his mother's words; he just repeated them. He didn't react to her touch.

"I love you. I love you. I love you." Spoken in his detached and strangely sincere way.

Johanna wiped tears from her cheek.

In the same sincere way, he asked, "Do you love me?"

She took a moment to think about that, but not for very long. "Yes. I think I do." Or she could come to love him, given some time. Not in the way Father had loved Mother.

Not in the way a brother would love a sister. But in a caring way. Roald was honest, simple-minded and immature most of the time, but completely sincere. He hated pomp and ceremony, and he hated being in the spotlight. The more pressure people put on him, the more strange things he did or said. He was odd, and unpredictable especially when provoked, but he was not dumb.

In the darkness, she reached up to him and stroked his cheek. The stubble of his beard scratched under her fingertips. Again, he didn't react, but she tried not to let that hurt her. *He doesn't know any better.*

What sort of upbringing had he received? How much had his mother and father hated him?

"Mistress Johanna? What are we going to do now?"

"Go to sleep, Nellie. We're not going anywhere tonight." And damn, she felt angry about that. She'd have to find another opportunity to escape in a place that was even further from the *Lady Sara*, from where the ship would be even harder to find. What if they arrived at the place where the bandits were taking them tomorrow morning?

The night was full of questions and no one had any answers. The bandits snored by the fire. The bears snored, too, and grunted occasionally, as if they were having a dream about . . . what did bears dream about?

Roald also fell asleep, a warm weight against her. He twitched occasionally. Nellie mumbled in her sleep. Johanna wasn't sure if Loesie was asleep, but every now and then, she spotted a faint glow of magic in the place where she had last seen Loesie. Little wisps that curled into the air. Once, she thought she could make out Loesie's cupped hands by the light of the faint glow. She tried to ignore it, but it scared her. If only she knew what was wrong with Loesie and what she could do about it.

She watched that spot of light, waiting for Loesie to do

something that would tell Johanna for sure that she was now possessed by an evil lord, but of course that would be all too convenient a thing to happen. It didn't.

Somehow, Johanna must have fallen asleep, because the dark forest bled into green pastures with cows, and happy farmers bringing cheeses to market. All the usual people were there: the clog-sellers at the markets, the silly nobles with their Lurezian fashion, and even Octavio Nieland, holding his wine glass by the stem with a gloved hand, giving her a look of superiority.

Was Octavio Nieland even still alive?

Nothing would ever be the same, ever again.

CHAPTER 4

THE NEXT MORNING dawned misty and bleak. Johanna woke up in the warmth of the blanket and Roald's body. Leaves and branches of the tree above her glistened with moisture. Occasionally drops fell to the forest floor. Their soft *plocks* were the only sounds in the muffled silence. She lifted her head. Roald was still asleep.

A lone figure stood at the bottom of the hill, looking over the misty glade where the horses grazed peacefully. Not a sign of last night's chaos remained. Johanna could make out some churned leaves at the bottom of the tree where they had sheltered last night, but that was all. That tree was so close to the camp that she was almost glad that the escape attempt hadn't been successful. In the mist the hounds and bears would have a huge advantage. They would never have gotten far.

The man looking over the glade turned around, and it was Sylvan. He proceeded to walk around the bottom of the hill, picking up sticks of wood as he went. He put these in a bag which he carried at his belt. The prick of magic hung in the air.

Something Kylian had said came to her mind. *We use magic at court.*

Clearly lots of people used magic for different things. It looked like Sylvan had set a magical ward to make sure that the prisoners didn't escape. Something that made people feel fear or reluctance to leave.

Nellie's behaviour from last night now made sense. As someone without magic, Nellie was more affected by the spell.

It also chilled Johanna to the core. Since the church forbade magic, no one in Saardam learned anything about it. She had always believed that magic happened by itself and you could read it, but not control it, but she was clearly wrong about that.

It looked like you could imbue the wood with images that made a person scared. What if you could make a person feel anything simply by leaving a piece of wood in a room?

Do you want to sell your business?

Buy my stock?

Marry my daughter?

She shivered. If she was right, people needed to learn about this magic, not run away from it, because entire countries could be controlled by it.

And then a thought: maybe entire countries were *already* controlled by it. Not Burovia, Gelre or Estland, where magic was more common, but Saarland.

Well, that was a very disturbing thought.

Johanna carefully wriggled out from under the blanket. Her muscles screamed protest from having sat in an uncomfortable position all night. Her bladder almost hurt from being too full.

A couple of the other bandits were already up. One of the nameless ones was cooking something in a pot over the fire with another one waving a blanket to fan the fire. The wood was obviously wet, because it produced a lot of smoke.

Johanna ducked behind the large tree. The bear lifted its head, but didn't get up. It was watching her.

Sylvan had disappeared around the corner of the hill, but Johanna held no illusions that he didn't know that she was here. Johanna wavered between seeing what he was doing and relieving herself, and nature won. Wetting herself would be very uncomfortable.

The trunk was wide enough for her to hide behind, but now the horses all stood watching her from the other side of the creek.

"Hey," Johanna whispered, and flapped her hand.

The horses didn't move.

"Scat!"

They just stared at her.

To her annoyance, another bandit had come to the creek to wash his face.

Well, it was not to be helped. Johanna pulled up her skirt but when she squatted to do her business, the man at the creek turned around. It was Ludo. His face split into a leery grin.

And she was to spend another day on a horse with this creep, trying to avoid his groping hands?

Sooner or later, something was going to break.

She remembered what Nellie had said about him last night and shuddered. If doing that thing with Roald hurt her, she could only imagine how much it would hurt for a man twice his size.

Ludo said something. She noticed his exceedingly hairy arms. She wondered if the rest of him—

No, this was definitely not a good thing to be thinking about right now.

"I'm married," she said, making her tone as vicious as she could make it.

Ludo laughed in a "like I care" manner, and went up the hill, hitching up his pants as he went.

By the time Johanna came back to the camp, the others were awake and one of the bandits was handing out dirty bowls containing a lumpy grey substance that did not deserve the word "porridge". He gave her a bowl.

It didn't look appetising, but it smelled of grain and her stomach probably wouldn't mind, as long as it was warm and filling.

As a bonus, too, Ludo sat on the other side of the fire and hadn't made a grab for Nellie.

There were no spoons, but it was so stiff that they could eat it with their fingers. Loesie did it with both hands, as if she hadn't eaten for days. Nellie did this daintily, with a prim expression on her face and not looking at anyone. Her face was very pale. Nellie's bonnet, normally pristine white, was grimy and dirty.

"I want honey," Roald said, poking at the contents of his bowl.

"There is no honey," Johanna said.

"It doesn't taste any good without honey."

"I know, but there is no honey." She knew she shouldn't let his stubbornness get to her, but a sudden wave of irritation made her grumpy.

"I got honey from the farm."

"Yes, but it's at the boat. We're not at the boat. Come, eat up."

Some of the bandits had already eaten and were rolling up their mats. Johanna dug into the sticky substance with her fingers. It was warm, but stuck to the inside of her mouth like glue. She struggled to swallow the stuff.

"I haven't said it yet today," Roald said.

"Said what?" She looked to the side, her mouth full of grainy sticky porridge that she was trying to work into her stomach.

"I love you."

It was the strangest thing someone had said to her while she was trying not to gag. His expression was so sincere that it made her choke up, which didn't help her ability to swallow gluey porridge. She couldn't speak, and brushed his hand with the fingers on her right hand, which weren't sticky.

Roald was so sincere, so innocent, she had to protect him from whatever the bandits had in store for them today. Most of all, she had to protect his identity.

Sigvald stood with his hands at his hips, watching his men. He and Sylvan exchanged meaningful looks, but said nothing. Johanna wondered about Sylvan's status. He seemed to be one of the youngest but was treated as one of the higher-ranking members of the group. She hadn't seen him eat breakfast, or eat last night. He hadn't taken part in sharing the liquor.

With his long plaits, tattoos and scar on his face, he looked creepy. His youth only accentuated the effect. He was too young to have a position of leadership in this group, so it had to have come from his other abilities.

Some of the bandits had already finished with breakfast, and one of those brought the horses back across the creek. The animals were restless, grumbling and nibbling at each other, and probably sensed that they were about to leave. When breakfast was done, the men finished packing and the first ones climbed on their horses. Four remained with saddles and without packs, one each for Johanna, Roald, Nellie and Loesie, with their riders. As she had expected, Johanna was paired with Ludo again. Just her luck.

The column set off through the forest at a plodding pace. They went around the course of the creek, past the ruins of the farm and the water mill. The giant wheel stood idle, with water cascading uselessly over the scoops. Some of them had been destroyed by fire.

From there they went up the next hill. Johanna noticed a sigil cut into the bark of a tree. A sign of ownership or direction? She studied the various tattoos and signs on jerkins or packs, but couldn't see the same sign anywhere. Was that a good thing?

Ludo behaved better than he had the previous day, perhaps because Sigvald stayed close. Maybe he had an interest in delivering the prisoners unharmed.

As the morning wore on, the mist lifted. Sunlight came through, casting brilliant rays of light through gaps in the foliage. Birds broke into unfamiliar songs, nothing like the sound of the larks, lapwings and sea birds that you would hear in the fields of Saarland. These birds sounded musical and melodious. Occasionally, Johanna would see a silhouette of a bird hopping about in the branches. Once she spotted a small bird on the ground, scurrying in the leaves. It was brown with a vivid orange chest. Roald would know what type of bird it was.

Around mid-morning, the lush beech trees made way for scrawny pines. The air had a curious smell here, and the ground underfoot became soft with springy moss, so that the horses' hooves made almost no noise. In places the soil had been churned over. Pigs did that, she remembered.

There were curious signs of previous human habitation: the occasional circle of wooden poles stood on the mossy ground, often surrounding a mossy mound. Mostly, the posts were badly decomposed and some had fallen into heaps, so whatever the posts were for, it had been a long time since people had lived in this area. There were no fields, no farms. The pines looked thin and emaciated. Their sparse foliage let through lots of light. Faint patches of mist still lingered near the ground, giving the forest an ethereal appearance.

The air pricked with magic. Even though these were not willow trees, Johanna had no doubt that they would have stories to tell of death and failure, of ghosts and magic. With the massacre the tree had shown her yesterday, it made her feel cold.

She shivered, despite the nice day.

They stopped for the midday meal in a mossy clearing with another one of those mounds surrounded by tree stumps. The men sat down on the moss.

Johanna's backside was so sore that she remained standing while she ate the dry bread the bandits gave her. Nellie complained, but both Roald and Loesie were quiet, each struggling with their own pain and fears.

Johanna eyed the mound. She took a chance and put her hand on a nearby tree, but all she saw was tranquil forest. Either her magic didn't extend to pine trees, or the images had faded. In most cases, with wood that was part of buildings, images lasted a few weeks, but much longer if no one touched the wood or nothing happened.

She leaned against the tree, studying the mound, noticing that no one, not even de dogs or bears, went inside the circle of posts.

"They're burial mounds," Roald said behind her.

"They must be very old."

"They are. It's been a long time since people lived here. The hunter tribes came here to flee the Westfalian invasion, but the land was too poor to support farming. People moved on to the low country or the river towns. Many people died of the plague while they lived here and they're all buried in the forest."

"I think their ghosts linger in this place."

"Ghosts are not real."

Johanna thought of the white horses she had seen last night. If they weren't ghosts, then what were they? "I think ghosts and magic are real. This place has a lot of magic. You can feel it in the way that it's so quiet here. The moss on the ground takes away all the sounds. Mist hangs between the trees like trails of magic. And then there are these burial mounds. Why did so many people die here while no one lives here now? Did they all just pack up and leave? Don't you think this forest is spooky?"

He frowned at her. Sometimes, when he spoke about all the things he knew, and when he was relaxed, it was easy to forget how awkward he was around people.

"I think it's spooky here," Nellie said. "You can feel it. It's as if the dead whisper in the back of your mind. I'll be glad when we come to civilisation."

Johanna wasn't sure if there *was* much civilisation out here.

"*She* doesn't like it here." She nodded at Loesie, who sat on the ground eating her bread. She didn't look at anyone else, and kept the chunk of bread close to her chest, as if afraid that someone would take it off her.

"Do you feel the magic, Loesie?"

"Ghghghghgh!"

Johanna searched for the other person with magic, Sylvan, but couldn't see him anywhere. Not with the young men, not with Sigvald, not with the horses. Sylvan's big black horse wasn't there either. When had he left?

His absence didn't seem to worry anyone. Sigvald was talking to the older man with the missing teeth and the younger bandits were sharing a joke of some sort.

Guess it had to be all right, then

"You're more familiar with that area than any of us, Roald. Do you have any idea where we are?"

He frowned at her. "I told you yesterday, we're close to Duke Lothar's land."

Not that she knew where that was. "Do you think they're taking us to the duke?"

"Duke Lothar does not let anyone on his land unless they're invited."

"That means yes?" Did that mean they were invited or they were about to run into an ambush?

"Surely the duke will realise his mistake and let us pass?" Nellie said.

"What is he supposed to mistake us for?" Having heard Roald's story about the royal family of Gelre, she hardly thought anyone would mistake the group for innocent travellers. She became increasingly sure that the duke was the boss of these bandits and had sent them with a reason.

A mild commotion behind them signalled Sylvan returning with three dead rabbits tied up by the back legs. His horse's flanks were moving fast and covered in sweat.

Sigvald made a sharp remark, to which Sylvan retorted with a toss of his head. Sigvald replied something about *You can be responsible for the trouble.*

Sylvan said under his breath, "Coward."

Sigvald leapt and pulled him by the leg of his trousers. Sylvan hadn't expected that and fell from the saddle on top of his attacker.

With shouts of protest, a couple of other bandits sprang forward and pulled the pair apart.

There was no time for this, one man said.

Another said that they'd all agreed on something.

A third said he had enough of the nonsense and wanted to go back. Back where, he didn't say or Johanna couldn't make out.

The men were all shouting at each other, filling the quiet forest with angry voices. Roald covered his ears with his hands, rocking from side to side. Johanna knelt next to him—

ouch, her backside—and tried to calm him down. He was humming to himself.

Johanna had to do something, or he would start banging his head against a tree trunk, so she started singing the words of a children's nursery rhyme, the only song she could remember.

He lowered his hands and listened to her. His face relaxed.

The argument between the bandits dissolved with the men talking to each other in small groups, with angry glances across the clearing. With Sigvald snapping harsh words at the prisoners that seemed to be about Roald, and sounded like an insult, but Johanna didn't catch the meaning. Perhaps it was better that she didn't.

The men climbed back on their horses and left the clearing split up into two distinct groups: those who agreed with Sigvald and those who wanted to go with Sylvan. Ludo rode with Sigvald, and so did the old bandit who rode with Loesie and the shy young man who shared his horse with Nellie, but Roald's bandit had changed camps.

This worried Johanna a lot. Sylvan and his group rode too far to the side for her to speak to Roald. The horse also moved too much for her to tell if he was rocking from side to side. The bandit would have told him to sit still. Roald was good at following orders, but he was going to be stressed. Not much disturbance was needed for him to throw a screaming fit. He'd been fragile enough at their last stop.

Whenever the two groups came close enough, he didn't make eye contact. Not a good sign, she thought. Maybe he thought the men were angry with him instead of each other. Maybe he didn't understand anger.

Each time Sylvan and his group rode further away, she was afraid that they would split up and go their own way. That fear clamped its cold fingers around her heart. They could not afford to lose Roald.

The vegetation now consisted of mainly pine trees, most of them twisted and knotted, with few healthy branches. Soon, the cover of trees stopped altogether to make way for a field of low shrubbery with the occasional straggly tree.

From the top of the horse, Johanna could see over many hills of it, dark green vegetation dotted with grazing sheep.

Was this the thing they called *heather*? Her mother used to speak of it a lot, because apparently there were big fields of it in northern Estland. Apparently at the end of summer, it bloomed purple. It was the beginning of summer now, still spring, really, so the hills were a dull dark green.

The group followed a track up one hill down the other side. It was more like a sheep track than a proper road, and it was narrow, so the horses walked in single file, Sigvald's group first and then Sylvan's group quite a way behind. Johanna couldn't even see Roald anymore, even though she risked Ludo's attention a few times by looking over her shoulder.

She listened, but heard nothing except the clop, clop, clop of the horses behind them, and the whistle of the wind, especially when they came to the hilltops.

The ground in the valleys was often wet, with scrawny black-and-white-trunked birch trees. Sometimes there was a little creek or pond; sometimes there was only tall grass. If one of the horses wanted a drink, its hooves churned up the soil, leaving deep tracks in the mossy ground.

After they had traversed a few such hills, the forest disappeared from sight.

The ground became increasingly barren, often with exposed patches of white sand on the surface between the shrubs. Sometimes the sand lay in little soft-looking mounds, with animal tracks across its surface; sometimes rainwater had etched deep ruts in the ground, and the jagged walls of earth would show sand of different colours, mostly white, light grey or rust.

Although the travelling party disturbed a few flocks of sheep, they saw no people. Once they passed an abandoned hut, its roof covered in dead heather plants which, apparently, the people had dug, with adhering soil and all, out of the surrounding hillsides. Next to it was a field where the churned soil was still visible, coated in a layer of loose sand. A soft, wind-blown hill of sand lay on the lee side of a timber structure that looked like a well. Sand had also heaped on the lee side of the farmhouse, and threatened to enter the structure's open door.

Johanna shuddered at the thought of what had happened to the inhabitants of the house. All signs of human habitation they had seen since being captured told a story of death and destruction. The burnt-out shell of the water mill, the burial mounds, and now this.

This land was so badly cursed that it sowed dissonance even in those who crossed it. Just look at how the bandits argued all the time.

Not much later, they crested the top of a hill, and the view forward as far as they could see consisted only of white sand.

Sigvald held up his hand. Horses stopped, with much blowing and snorting. Sigvald spoke to the bandit next to him, but they were too far away for Johanna to hear what was said.

They waited. Not a word was exchanged. Horses tossed heads and shook manes. They sniffed the air.

On the horizon to the left and behind, a bank of sharp-edged clouds towered into the sky, topped by a great wedge-shaped protrusion. The sky above was still blue, but the air had taken on that oppressive quality that preceded bad weather.

Sylvan and his group came up from behind. Johanna was glad to see Roald, and glad that he didn't seem to have thrown a screaming fit, although he kept moving his head from side to side.

The bandits went into a discussion which Johanna thought was about which direction to travel. Several men didn't like the sand. Sylvan said to keep going. Sigvald didn't like that either. Johanna suspected that Sigvald didn't like *anything* that Sylvan suggested, but they seemed to reach some sort of agreement.

Sylvan slid from his horse and took it by the reins. He led the animal onto the sand, straight past Sigvald, who said nothing and stood with his hands crossed over his chest.

Sylvan stopped at the crest of the nearest dune, looked at the sky and waved his free hand. A gust of wind whipped up sand around him. He stood with his eyes closed and his hands spread, palms out.

Wind magic.

The men in his group were also getting off their horses. The old bandit had already lifted Loesie down. She stood with her arms clamped around herself as if she were cold. *She also feels the magic.*

Johanna refused Ludo's help in getting down, and so did Nellie. Johanna managed to get down from the horse safely, but Nellie half-fell and landed clumsily. Fortunately the sand was soft and nothing was hurt except Nellie's pride.

Still brushing the sand off her clothes, Nellie joined Johanna and Roald. "What are we doing? Why did we get off here?"

Sylvan turned around. "Too hard for the horses to carry us. We walk them."

"Are we near the sea?" Nellie asked.

This was like the sand dunes near the ocean in Saarland, only at the ocean there was one row of dunes and then the beach, but here there seemed to be no end to the expanse of sand. Johanna didn't *think* there was an ocean on the other side, because Gelre was a land-locked country and the northern ocean was to the north of Estland. But to be honest, she didn't understand why this sand was here either.

It's a cursed country. That was all she knew.

The group started across the sand in single file. Sylvan went first with his horse, the two bears and the dogs, then Sigvald and a couple of his men leading their horses, then Roald, Johanna, Nellie and Loesie, and finally the rest of the group and remaining horses.

The air became more pressing, while thunder growled in the distance. The horses were skittering, lifting heads and tossing manes. Father always said it was a bad thing to be caught in a field during a storm.

The wind blew in squalls.

Sand whipped around them, biting into exposed skin. But it was more than sand that caused Johanna's skin to tingle. There was *magic* in the air.

Even the hounds stayed close to the group. They whined and squeaked with tails tucked between their legs and preferred to walk between the horses. The bears stopped every so often to sniff the air.

Sand got in Johanna's shoes, in her eyes and in her hair. It bit in the exposed parts of skin. The wind swelled until it took Johanna's breath away and carried sand over the surface in streaks

Sigvald hurried the group along. The horses plodded through the biting sand with their heads held low.

Johanna had to force herself to put one foot in front of the other. Every time she thought they were at the end of this horrible sand, there was another hill. They would sink deep into the sand on the lee side, ploughing through it almost up to her knees.

Nellie collapsed several times, and cried that she didn't want to keep going, but each time a bandit hauled her to her feet, increasingly roughly.

Johanna wanted to shout, *Stop the theatrics. It's not helping.* But she said nothing for fear of getting a mouth full of sand.

Loesie plodded on, her eyes closed. Her mouth moved, as if she was praying.

Roald seemed the only one unaffected. His hair whipped across his face, but his expression was blank as usual.

On and on they went.

Thunder was now close enough to make the air shake. The dogs yowled, and Sylvan yelled at them while trying to keep his horse quiet.

The muscles in Johanna's legs screamed from exhaustion. The wind picked up and blew lashes of sand against her that bit even through her clothes. Sand got under her dress. It got in her eyes and her mouth. She could barely open her eyes to see.

What sort of terrible evil country was this?

CHAPTER 5

T HE STORM broke with a few claps of thunder that made the ground shake. A sharp burst of rain halted the drifting sand. The wind stopped as suddenly as it had come. The sky cleared with crisp clouds and even a few patches of blue. The rain had made the sand wet and easier to walk on. The magic had vanished from the air.

Coming over the crest of a particularly tall dune, Johanna spotted a dark row of forest on the horizon, a wonderful sight after all that loose sand and the dunes.

A quick look over her shoulder revealed an untouched landscape of white sand dunes with a few gnarly pine trees. The wind had erased all their tracks.

After crossing a few more dunes, they came to a small village, nested in an alcove between sand dunes that smothered a landscape of heather and small pine trees.

The houses were low structures from rough wood, with no windows, half-sunken in the ground. Like the abandoned house they had seen previously, their slanting roofs were covered with sods of heather, the branches brown and dead, and now all quite sandy from the wind. Johanna counted twelve such houses, each of them surrounded by fields with the most miserable crops that Johanna had ever seen. The plants were pale green, almost yellow, their stems short and uneven, and very sparse. Not even the weeds had made much of an appearance.

A couple of women were working in a field, scooping off encroaching sand and carting it out of the settlement in a wheelbarrow. A small sad-looking paddock with a rickety barn held an ox and a shaggy-haired pony. A man was filling the drinking trough that stood against the barn wall. Two children herded a group of sheep along the main "road", a path pockmarked with puddles and rutted with tracks from nothing but wheelbarrows.

Someone whistled and everyone in the village turned around to watch the newcomers. People stared at the horses. Even if they weren't being ridden, the bandits' horses looked magnificent compared to the village animals.

A couple of scrawny children stood in the doorway of the closest house, dirty, dressed in rags, very skinny and small.

In the centre of the village, a man with a shovel in his hand came out of a barn as the procession came to a stop on what looked like a village square. Sigvald handed the reins of his horse to the young bandit next to him and went to speak to this villager. Sigvald was much taller and broader than the man, and his tattooed head gave him an imposing appearance.

They exchanged greetings, the villager appearing very timid. He didn't look Sigvald in the eye.

His hands were dirty, and when he wiped his face he spread a smudge over his forehead.

A couple of small boys stared at the party from the barn door behind him. A young woman dragged them out of the way with a hissed, "Begone with you, or the magician will change you into a toad."

Sigvald said something about a bed and food.

The man flinched. "The barn is available, as always. But, Lord, we have barely enough to feed ourselves. The winter has not been kind to us."

His speech sounded a bit odd and old-fashioned, but it was surprising how well Johanna understood him, better than she understood the bandits.

Sigvald shouted at him about having an agreement. The man retreated further, muttering about poor harvests and fields being covered in sand. "It's like a curse, my lord."

"You deserve it," Sigvald said.

"We bring our own food." Sylvan came forward, holding up the rabbits. "If you can cook them."

The man's eyes widened. "Yes, yes, certainly, lord. Lenie, put them over the fire and ready the barn."

The young woman scurried forward, took the rabbits and disappeared after the two boys. Sigvald gave Sylvan a dirty look. Sylvan said something in too low a voice for Johanna to hear and Sigvald replied with an obscenity.

"We will tend to your horses," the villager said.

"Make sure they're well-looked after." Sigvald's voice was a growl.

"Certainly, my lord." He called a few names.

A couple of men came out from the other huts. All of them were skinny, with bony arms and hollow cheeks. They took the horses to the pen near the village's well, which was occupied by the pony and the ox. The horses bunched together in the corner furthest away from those two animals. They held their heads low and showed little interest in their companions. The sand had exhausted them as well.

One man dragged in a wooden trough, while a young woman came to the well.

She lowered the bucket, keeping a wary eye on Sigvald. Johanna could hear the bucket hitting water, not very deep.

The woman turned the wheel to bring the bucket up with a squeak, squeak, squeak that sounded ominous in the silence. She emptied the bucket in the trough. The water had a red-brown tinge.

Sigvald snorted. "That's not water, that's piss."

She flinched away from him. "This is the only water we have, my lord."

Johanna cringed at how these people treated him as a highly-ranked person.

The girl trembled visibly when she lowered and pulled up the bucket for the second time. Squeak, squeak, squeak went the wheel into that tense silence. She emptied it in the water trough. *Splash*. The horses gathered around.

"Wait," Sylvan said. He pushed himself between the horses' bodies and stuck his hand in the water. He paused, with his eyes closed. To an outsider, it might have looked like he relished the coolness, but Johanna could read the signs.

Water magic. She'd thought he had wind magic. Was it even possible to have two different kinds of magic in one person?

He turned to Sigvald and nodded. He had judged the water safe. The horses drank and not much later, the dogs and the bears came to join them. The girl brought up a few more buckets of water, doing her best to ignore the gazes of Ludo and several other bandits. A young boy brought a wheelbarrow full of hay.

"I wonder where they cut the hay in this miserable place." Sigvald lifted his face to Sylvan, as if his question was a challenge.

Sylvan snorted, but said nothing.

Someone was spoiling for a fight, but Johanna had no idea what it was about.

Sigvald went inside the barn when the owner called him. The rest waited around uneasily. A couple of the children stared at the group from the door of another house. Johanna met the eyes of a little girl and found herself the subject of the stares of all the children. Most were scrawny, dirty. One had a funny eye that looked in the wrong direction; another's foot was turned awkwardly inwards.

She felt too embarrassed for words. She didn't want to be part of this group that barged into this poor village and demanded favours that the villagers couldn't afford.

Never had Johanna seen poverty like this. There were beggars and refugees in Saardam. Some were sick or had lost limbs in wars, but even if they couldn't find work, there was the church where the poor and destitute could always get food. Even in their plain farm clothes, dirty and tired as they were, the Saarlander travellers looked so much richer.

The farmer called the group into the barn. Johanna, Roald, Nellie and Loesie followed the bandits through a rickety door into the hastily vacated room.

A few lights burned on roughly-hewn pillars that supported the roof. The floor was covered in heather twigs in a layer so thick it was springy. Rough-hewn wooden planks held up the layer of soil on the roof, but some of the roots had worked their way between the planks and dangled from the ceiling like spider webs. It was surprisingly warm in here. The bandits put down their packs along the side wall. All the saddles and riding tack went near the door.

"The food will be out shortly," the farmer said to Sigvald.

There was a rough door in the back wall that opened a sliver, and the two boys peeped through again.

The farmer turned to them. "Hide yourselves. Don't annoy our guests."

But now the door opened further, and two teenage boys entered carrying a table, which they placed in the middle of the barn. Then the little ones carried in a bench which they placed on one side of the table. They ran back to fetch another bench for the other side of the table. The older ones brought a couple of rough-made chairs that went on both ends of the table. Sigvald sat in one of them, Sylvan in another.

There was not enough room for everyone, and a couple of younger bandits, as well as the prisoners, had to sit on the ground.

Johanna, Nellie, Roald and Loesie ended up next to the saddles, which exuded the smell of horse.

The bandits laughed and talked as if they owned this place and it was their right to be here.

The farmer, whose name appeared to be Otto, called into the adjacent room, "Bring the soup now, Lenie."

Johanna revised her assessment of these people. While this was obviously a barn, the sheep were outside at this time of the year, and the family made money by offering travellers a simple place to stay. She guessed there hadn't been any travellers for a long time. Who would willingly traverse that horrible sand?

The farmer's daughter brought in a large pan of soup that smelled wonderful, which she set on the table with the announcement, "The rabbits will be awhile cooking."

She first served the bandits, starting with Sigvald, and only came to Johanna, Roald, Nellie and Loesie when she had finished with all of the men.

She handed Johanna a battered bowl, their eyes meeting. Lenie's eyes were grey, and she wore her hair tied back in a severe bun that made her look much older than she was. "I didn't know that women rode with Sigvald."

"We're not part of his group," Johanna said, well aware that that Sigvald had his head turned and was listening while pretending to talk to his fellows.

"You're travellers?"

"Prisoners. We're from Saardam."

The girl's eyes widened. "Really? The home of the free church?"

Free Church? "We have the Church of the Triune."

"That's it." She lowered her voice, "We're Free Church members, too. That's why we can't live in Florisheim. You know how they allow magic over there?" She glanced at the bandits. Some had finished their soup.

One of them yelled, "Stop talking, serve us first!"

The girl turned away. "I'm sorry, I've got to go. Will you pray with us later tonight? It would be an honour."

"Hurry up!" Sigvald yelled and another bandit hit the table with a thud.

The girl went back inside and made her round past everyone at the table with a pan of mash.

Johanna watched her sinewy arms as she lifted the heavy pan. She was really incredibly skinny. The Church of the Triune? Here? Really?

When the girl got to Ludo, he squeezed her behind. She shied away from him.

She finished her round and came back with bowls for Johanna, Nellie, Roald and Loesie.

"Be careful of that one," Johanna said in a low voice, glancing at Ludo. "He's been harassing us the entire journey. Don't give him ideas."

The girl gave her a strange look. She picked up her pan and walked out without a further word. No thanks, no questions.

Oh well, at least she'd warned the girl.

The soup was watery, the bread made without butter or salt and the plates were stained and chipped. The rabbit was a little undercooked and the mash very bland. But it was warm and filled her belly for at least a little while. She met Nellie's eyes over the top of Nellie's bowl. "You're all right?"

Nellie nodded. Her cheeks were red from being outside all day.

Both Loesie and Roald had finished their meals. Loesie lay curled up with her head on her hands, not unlike a cat. Her eyes were closed. Roald leaned back against one of the saddles, also with his eyes closed. His mouth was slightly open.

Exhausted. Johanna felt like joining them.

"Isn't it terrible how these people live?" Nellie said softly. "They go to church and are good and honest people."

Johanna wasn't sure if going to church was a quality that defined a good person, but she wasn't going to argue.

From her position she could see through the open door into the other half of the house. There was a single room, now empty in the middle where the table would normally go. In the corner stood a simple stove, where the girl was just putting a block of wood on the fire. The two little boys sat on the ground playing a game by the light from the flames. A smoky rush light burned on a shelf, giving off only a faint glow.

The girl beckoned Johanna to come. The bandits had finished their meal and had taken out the flask again, talking and laughing.

"Come," she said to Nellie. Best to let Roald and Loesie sleep.

Johanna and Loesie had to step over Roald's outstretched legs to get to the door. Sylvan's glare followed them all the way.

The other room was possibly even darker than the barn. Apart from the open stove, there was little furniture. The bandits were using the only table and chairs these people possessed. There were a number of beds around the room's perimeter. One of Lenie's adolescent brothers lay in a bed, looking at the fire. The other sat playing a game with his two young brothers near the stove lit by the glow from the fire.

In the far corner of the room was a small altar with whittled pieces of wood and oddly-shaped stones. A particularly knotty piece of wood looked like a round-waisted woman. Maybe a goddess of fertility. They would need one here.

There was also a stone with a hole in the middle and a blackened tooth. Not human, not like any animal that lived on land. Johanna had sometimes seen teeth like these on fish, but this one was much bigger. Other items included a stick with a plume made from feathers, dangling on a string made from horsehair. Johanna was unfamiliar with the type of bird —it had feathers with light and dark blue spots. She touched the colourful feathers.

"It's for reading the wind," Lenie said.

"Wind magic?"

She frowned. "We do not use that word. The church does not allow magic. Magic is the evil that the duke's men wreak upon us."

"But the wind shows you what's happening in another place?"

The girl frowned at her. "You know this also?"

"Yes, we do." *And we call it magic.* "I don't see things on the wind. I see things in wood."

Johanna put her hand on the figure of the wooden woman. It was pine, but she'd grown used to the fact that in these parts, all wood showed her things, not just willow. It showed her the family gathered around the altar. In the vision, Lenie lit a candle with a burning stick, a proper candle and not one of the horribly smoky rush lights. That candle must have been a real treasure.

There was also another woman, holding the statue in her hands. She was older, with wisps of grey hair, and very pregnant.

Lenie's mother, who had died recently in childbed? Lenie and her four brothers were the only ones in the room. The mother would be here if she were alive.

Johanna cringed inside.

Lenie continued, "The wind tells us when people come or when rain comes. There is always wind here. Without reading of the wind, we could never survive."

They were barely surviving as it was. These people were so poor that she couldn't imagine it. The land was poor, and the fields could never grow much with the battle against the sand. They even had to trade in their dignity by letting a bunch of rogue bandits use their only table.

"Why don't you move into the forest?" Johanna asked.

"Oh no, that's the duke's land. We can't go there."

"If you offer to work for the duke, wouldn't he allow you to live on his land? You could work on his fields or—"

"No, never. These rich people blame the sand curse on us. They say that wherever we go we bring it with us, because we belong to the Free Church. They use magic and call us mad. They would kill us if we went on their land."

"Have you tried?"

"Many people have. Sometimes we are hungry and don't have enough to eat, especially when winter comes. Sometimes the boys go into the forest to trap rabbits. Other times, people go into the forest to trade things, but they never come back. We've lost many precious possessions that villagers have taken to sell at the markets in return for food. Wherever we go, we always have to cross the duke's land, and no one goes there and comes back."

Johanna imagined the strip of forest as she had seen it before coming into the village. It was just a forest, right? "What do you think happens to those people?" She shivered. There was no such thing as *just a forest*. Forests were full of evil.

"We don't know. Sometimes we see creatures amongst the trees."

"Creatures? Like the bears the bandits have?"

"Them, and others. Sometimes they're people, sometimes they're . . . something else. Magical, evil. The duke is a bad magician."

She let a silence lapse. A chill crept over Johanna's back. People in Saardam didn't believe in magic because they never saw any, because there were no forests in Saarland.

She asked, "What causes the drifting sand?"

"It's a punishment from the True God. Eventually, the sand will batter against the duke's evil magic long enough to break through his defences. Then he will be drowned under huge mountains of sand. You must pray with us and maybe we can make it happen."

Johanna wasn't going to tell the girl that her "Free Church" and the Church of the Triune sounded like very different institutions, or that the Church of the Triune in Saarland considered the ability of being able to see things in the wind or in wood as magic. Their "True God" was probably also not the same as the Triune.

She said nothing about some of those "evil magicians" being right here in the house, in the group of bandits whom they treated as guests. Anyone who knew about magic could see it in Sylvan's eyes.

She was not even going to say anything about the sand not being their friend, and if anyone was going to drown in it, the people in this village would be the first to go.

When you were this poor, there were no easy options.

She sat with Lenie on her knees in front of the altar.

Nellie had taken off her bonnet, and to be honest, it was so dirty she looked much better without it.

Lenie started the prayer in a low voice.

"True God, hear our prayers. We pray for our forefathers

and all those who have been taken from us. We pray for our granpa and granma and our ma and our little sister who never took any steps with her little feet. We pray for Jan because his wife is sick, and for Seb, who is still missing two of his sheep. We pray that they may be found. We pray that the harvest might be good this year and that we have enough to eat through winter. We pray for the visitors and their safety, that they will make it safely through the duke's land. We pray that the day will come that magic is defeated and our land will be free of the sand curse." She fell silent and no one said anything for a while.

Then she turned to Johanna. "What do you pray?"

The question hit Johanna in her heart. She started in a low voice. "I pray for my country where many people were killed by fire and fire demons. I pray that whatever evil destroyed Saardam has been defeated. I pray that there are people braver than us who fought the invasion. I pray that my father has survived. . . ." She had to stop speaking because her voice would no longer cooperate. Then she steeled herself. "I pray for my husband who needs all the help he can get to—" She almost said *reign the country* but remembered that no one was to know who they were. "—to help put the country back in order. I pray that I will have the strength to help him."

"I didn't know you were married," Lenie said.

"He's asleep in the other room."

"The young man with the beard?" Lenie frowned. "I thought he was . . ."

"He was what?"

"He's not really normal, is he?"

"Normal enough." Seriously, she was getting annoyed with people pointing out the obvious. "He is awkward around people." And that, when she came to think of it, was a very good description of what ailed Roald. He didn't like people and didn't know how to talk to people except when he was talking about things he knew. He didn't like crowds, didn't like standing out or speaking in public. Didn't like being the centre of attention. He couldn't tell emotions from a person's face. He didn't know "appropriate". When someone forced him to do things he hated or felt insecure doing, he behaved strangely.

It was now Nellie's turn for her prayers. In a soft voice, she said, "Like Johanna I pray for my country and the people in Saardam. I pray that they have the strength to recover and I pray that we will soon be with them again. I pray for my family, my father and mother and for my little brothers. . . ." Her voice wavered with emotion. "I pray for our Reverend Romulus, that he may have survived the cowardly attack and continues to help the common people of Saardam." Her eyes met Johanna's. Tears glittered in them. "I pray for our royal family, and that they will have the strength and support to once again make Saardam a peaceful place again."

"Please, Nellie," Johanna whispered. The royal family wasn't doing any such thing at the moment. The fact that she was now part of that family pressed heavily on her conscience. They should go back to what was left of Saardam as soon as possible. They had been planning to return the moment they were captured but, due to that misfortune, were still moving further and further away from the place where they should be.

The room blurred with the haze of tears.

Lenie, of course, didn't know what had happened in Saardam so Johanna told her as much as she knew, leaving out the parts about the royal family and Roald's identity. The four boys were listening, and while the younger ones wouldn't understand much, the older ones might.

Lenie turned her head as if to listen for something outside. "You better go back to the barn. My pa has gone to help one of the neighbours. He won't be happy if he sees me talking to you."

The reasons for parents to say things like that baffled Johanna endlessly, but she was too tired to argue. Too tired, in fact, for pretty much anything.

CHAPTER 6

BACK IN the other room, the bandits were singing and laughing like stupid oafs. They were telling jokes, most of them red-cheeked and bright-eyed from the liquor.

All except Sylvan, who sat at the corner of the table, meeting Johanna's eyes when she came back into the barn.

Lenie followed them to collect the plates, bowls and spoons. Johanna spotted her talking to Ludo. She smiled at him.

Johanna wanted to scream, *Don't give that creep ideas*, but there was little she could do.

Lenie left the room again, and came back to collect more plates. She smiled across the table at Ludo.

Johanna cringed and hoped the girl's father would come in soon. She was too innocent and too young to know what he wanted. If the bandits groped the daughter of their host, she didn't know how things would end. She was too tired to pack up and leave again. Too tired to face a duke with evil magic.

The barn door opened, and the farmer Otto came in. He

spotted his daughter talking to Sigvald and jerked his head to the other room.

Lenie scurried back into the family's room.

Johanna had trouble keeping her eyes open. Her position, leaning against the warmth of Roald's body, became comfortable and familiar.

Loesie had rolled onto her back, her arm stretched out over her head. Her hand twitched occasionally.

Otto spoke with Sigvald and then Ludo. They seemed to be negotiating, probably the price for their meal and stay. Johanna was too tired to listen. She leaned on one elbow in the heather twigs. The ground was surprisingly soft.

The farmer's four sons sat against the wall, watching the bandits. When had they been allowed to come in and what were they doing here?

Johanna dozed off, but next thing she noticed was Ludo leaving the room for the family's living quarters. The door shut behind him.

In one moment, Johanna was wide awake.

Lenie was in that room, Ludo had just gone in. Lenie's brothers were in the barn, and Otto was still talking to Sigvald. Was this what she thought it was?

She let her hand hover over the wood at her back, the planks whose other side formed the wall in the living room, but then she looped her arms around her drawn-up knees as tight as she could. She didn't want to know and didn't need to see.

A wave of hot anger took hold of her.

That filthy swine of a father of hers still talked to Sigvald, as if selling his daughter to bandits was the most normal thing in the world. Did he even know what this meant to her? She would never get married, never be wanted by a man, never be worth anything.

It seemed like Johanna watched the door forever. She

listened to the roaring of blood in her ears. Her backside got sore from sitting in the cramped position. She put one hand on Roald's shoulder and felt the steady rise and fall of his body with his breaths. A few days ago, she had felt sorry for "sacrificing" herself for the kingdom, but she had been so self-absorbed that she couldn't even see how rich she was. Her "sacrifice" would be another girl's dream.

Finally the door opened and Ludo came out. He had the nerve to grin at his comrades.

While he took his place at the table, another bandit went in.

Otto continued talking to Sigvald. The four boys sat and watched, their faces pale and gaunt.

They knew what was going on. *They* didn't like it.

The second man was back fairly quickly and then, fortunately, the four brothers went back into the room.

Their father stayed a little longer, after receiving a handful of coins from Sigvald. Going out the door, his eyes met Johanna's. She gave him the vilest stare she could muster. These people called themselves honest and religious? The same church as the Church of the Triune? No way.

The door shut.

Johanna let her shoulders slump.

Then again, it was easy for her to judge. If her family was as poor and desperate as these people, they might have done the same.

Even women of ill repute are people. She thought of Helena in Saardam, and her infectious laugh and endless source of gossip. To be honest, she preferred Helena to some of the "proper" nobles.

The boys removed the table and benches again and the bandits rolled out their mats. The farmer took the oil light into the other room. When he shut the door behind him, the barn became shrouded in darkness.

Soon, heavy breathing indicated that the bandits were asleep. One of the men started snoring, and then another. A horse made a snorting noise outside and a sheep bleated. One of the dogs grumbled in response.

Johanna fell asleep briefly, but she dreamed of climbing up a steep hill of drifting sand. With each step she took, more sand would cascade down from the top. It reached to her ankles, and then her knees, and then her thighs and her waist. She jerked awake, her heart thudding like crazy. Something heavy and warm lay over her: Roald's arm had fallen across her legs.

Johanna pushed the arm and hot blanket off her and lay staring at the darkness where the ceiling would be if she could see it.

The sighs of the wind over the roof made soft whispering sounds. They were like voices just out of hearing, voices that whispered warnings or spells, but could only be understood by people who had wind magic. Clearly the villagers could hear and see things in the wind, but all its secrets were kept from her.

The more she learned about magic, the more she realised that she knew nothing at all and that her own ability was paltry and insignificant. Maybe the people of the village were right in not considering the ability to see things on the wind and in wood proper magic. No one could do anything with the ability, except leave objects in places and retrieve them later to "read" them. It wasn't an active skill.

These people had experience with far more magic than she had seen in her lifetime.

Sylvan used kinds of magic she had never even known existed.

She remembered the ghost horses in the forest, the images of the murdered farmer and his family, the wrecked water mill. Wherever these men went, they killed and raped and pilfered as they pleased. It was a wonder that the four of them were still alive, a wonder that the men hadn't ripped the clothes off any of them.

That left only one option: their leader wanted them unscathed. She knew almost for certain that this leader was the duke who had tried to murder his half-brother the baron. She wasn't sure whether wanting the group alive was a good or bad thing. Did she really want to be confronted with the man who may have ordered the burning of Saardam? Who had sown death and destruction all the way down the river, just so that he could—what exactly? Was the whole thing about a feud between two half-brothers? She found that hard to believe.

She didn't know anymore. She was not too sure if she wanted to know. The duke might be the necromancer.

Had King Nicholaos really been so stupid as to approach a dark magician to try and bring Celine back from the dead?

Was the reason that the bandits had not tried to find out their names that they already knew? The necromancer might want to exact revenge on the last remaining survivor of the Carmine house.

And since Johanna was certain that there would not yet be an heir, the house that had brought peace to Saardam would die, and war would break out all over again. The Saardam nobles would fight. They had the money to put together an army. In fact, the king had been talking about that even before the burning.

They might fight over religion if the Church of the Triune appointed a governor. They might fight over rights of inheritance if one of the King's hated cousins tried to claim Saardam as his.

Under the king, Saardam had become important as port city. Maybe even Estland or Burovia would try to claim

Saardam to stabilise their access to luxury spices and tobacco, which the rich had so come to appreciate.

Johanna's thoughts went around and around in circles, and each time she revisited a particular line of thought, the ominousness of it seemed to have exploded until her thoughts were one big black pool of swirling evil magic.

They had to get away.

That thought was clear as glass to her. Roald could *not* fall into the hands of this duke.

But how? This was a stupid place for trying to escape, far more stupid than the forest of last night. The sand would show every footstep, and would slow them down. They'd spent half a day plodding through the sand, and it would be easy for nimble, able riders and dogs to catch up.

We could go into the forest.

She shuddered at the thought, but the bandits might not expect their captives to flee in that direction.

The saddles were right behind her. They would have to take horses, which were neatly stabled in the pen outside, and then ride until they came to a town. Florisheim, perhaps. That was where the baron had his castle, and the baron would be an enemy of the duke, if Roald's information was correct. If the baron and his son had survived the fire—and she had to assume that or all would be lost—they would have returned home by now.

Yes. That was probably their best chance. What was more, Sylvan had not gone outside after dinner, and would not have put his ward around the barn—probably because the people in the village would notice and would refuse to shelter "evil wizards"?

How to get to Florisheim? Turn west and find the river. Then follow it upstream. It would not be the shortest route, but one the bandits wouldn't expect them to take. They would expect them to go back to the *Lady Sara.*

Johanna rose, carefully, trying not to make any twigs crack.

Roald still lay as a warm presence next to her. She tapped him on the shoulder until he moved.

"Wha—?"

"Shhh." She whispered at the place where she thought his ear to be, "We escape."

"Ohh, I like tha—"

"Shhh. Be quiet." Was it possible for him to whisper?

One of the bandits gave a particularly noisy snore. Johanna held her breath, but his breathing settled again.

She bent over and whispered in the hollow between Roald's shoulder and his ear. "Stay here. Grab a saddle behind you. Wait until I say we're ready to go."

Next, she found Nellie, who woke with a gasp. "What?"

"Shhh. Get up." Fortunately, Nellie didn't protest.

Johanna crawled to Nellie's other side. "Loesie?" She shook Loesie's shoulder, disturbed at how bony she felt through her clothes.

"Hmmmm."

"Come. Be quiet."

As silently as she could, Johanna gathered up the blankets, draped them over the saddle that she picked up, and crept towards the barn door. The gear was so heavy that her arms were screaming. She had to put the saddle down to lift the wooden bar that locked the door. It creaked when she pushed it open and one of the dogs on the other side gave a warning *woof*.

Johanna froze, waiting for the racket of barks that would surely follow. But the dogs only squeaked, sticking their noses through the gap between the door and the doorframe and the saddle.

She stood still for a long time, but nothing moved. She let the hounds sniff her hand and the familiar smell of the saddle.

A tail went *thud, thud, thud* against the outside of the barn wall.

Johanna pushed the door open further and wriggled through, coming out in the cooler night air. The night was clear and the whole sky was so bright with stars that she could see the dark shapes of the dogs by starlight. The sky was never as clear as this in the hazy air of the coast. You could see all the constellations against the firmament of stars, a pale white band that arced across the sky. The moon had only just risen over the horizon, and its low light silvered the trees at the edge of the plain. Johanna waited outside the door until the others came through. The dogs crowded around her. She scratched their heads and behind their ears. In return they slobbered all over her hands.

Roald came out after her, yawning audibly, followed by Nellie. Johanna pushed the door shut after Loesie came out. They walked a little away from the barn, followed by the dogs. The bears were nowhere in sight.

"Where do we go?" Nellie whispered.

"Get the horses," Johanna said.

"And then? I don't want to go back through all that sand."

"We're not. We go through the forest. We ride like crazy until we get to Florisheim."

"Ghghghghgh!" Loesie said and her voice sounded stressed.

"We have no choice," Johanna said. "Quick. Roald, you know how to handle horses." She hoped he understood, because there wasn't the time to explain. She hoped Loesie wasn't going to do anything strange, because they couldn't afford to slow down.

The horses stood in the pen near the well, a mass of subtly shifting, breathing darkness. Johanna wondered why they hadn't been allowed to roam like the previous night.

Maybe Sigvald was afraid that they would get stolen, or maybe there was *something* out there that might eat horses.

When Johanna came closer to them, one snorted nervously.

Roald slipped past her, carrying his saddle and blanket.

"Be careful," she said. "They're very big."

"I know about horses."

She hoped he was right. He climbed over the fence and disappeared into that dark mass of animals.

They waited. The night was breathless and chilly. An eerie birdcall echoed in the still air. Nellie's teeth chattered.

"You're cold?"

"Yes. Nervous. I really need to visit the outroom."

"When we're out of here."

Roald also seemed to have quite good night vision, because not much later, he emerged from the group of horses leading an animal by the reins. He opened the gate to the pen and deposited those reins in her hand. It was one of the smaller packhorses.

"Here, hold on tight." He ducked back.

Johanna held on, but the horse was nervous, jiggling and pulling at the reins. The bears were somewhere around here, too, and if this horse kept going like this, the dogs would start barking and then everyone would come out.

Roald brought two more horses, giving the reins to Nellie.

"How are we going to get on their backs," Nellie said through her chattering. "They're so big."

"We'll have to walk the horses out and climb on once we get to the forest. We'll have to walk really slowly, or everyone will hear them."

Roald came with the last horse. "I'll leave the gate open."

That was a good idea. If the bandits woke up and discovered the horses loose, it would take them a while to find out that some were missing.

"Let's go," Johanna whispered. She was looking around for the bears but didn't see them anywhere.

But the horses saw *something*. Her horse was snorting and tossing its head. Another horse whickered in the dark.

Nellie squeaked.

"Calm down. I'll take these two." Roald took the reins from her. He was really quite good at this practical stuff. This place where he had spent the last few years sounded more like a religious farm.

Johanna turned her horse away from the houses of the village. There was now barely enough moonlight to see the outlines of the forest in the distance.

"They'll see our tracks in the morning," Nellie whispered behind her.

"Yes, but we'll ride soon. Once we're in the forest, our tracks will be less easy to see."

They walked quietly in single file. Johanna desperately wanted to go faster, but couldn't, because the horses would make too much noise. They now went up the sand hills and no one had breath for speaking. The horses seemed to have settled and plodded along peacefully.

Johanna could barely believe it, but it started to look like they had finally escaped.

Fields with crops stretched out on both sides of the path, probably oats and barley, but it was too dark to see.

They stopped at the edge of the field where the village was barely visible. The moon had risen over the trees and cast pale light over the world. The forest was a dark wall to their left, silent and brooding. There was not a breath of wind, but Johanna thought she could hear the leaves rustle.

The ghosts are already talking about us. Johanna shivered. All evil magic came from forests, she was sure about that.

Roald went around the horses to fasten and check the saddles on all of them. "Eastern saddles," he said. "I know how they work." He went back to his horse, and swung himself up.

Johanna tried to do the same, but oh, that awkward dress, and this horse was absolutely *huge*. There was no bandit to help her up. Nellie was struggling as well.

Johanna went to help her first and managed to push Nellie on top of the horse, but it fidgeted, and Johanna had to keep hold of the reins. Nellie was not a rider and might have ridden a pony maybe once or twice. She had to hitch her dress up high and now the horse wouldn't stand still for Nellie to get used to it.

"It's so tall. I'm afraid to fall off. I don't know that I can ride that well."

"Neither can I. Just do the best you can."

Just as well Roald had chosen the packhorses. Imagine what those giant black beasts would be like with clumsy riders.

Roald's horse didn't fidget. It stood perfectly still, its ears pricked forward. Roald was a silhouette in the saddle, sitting straight-backed.

With a lot of effort, Johanna managed to clamber up her own horse. "Ready to go, everyone?"

Loesie still stood next to the horse, silhouetted in the moonlight. Her hair was a tangled mess and the moonlight made the outline of it glow like silver. *Like a ghost*.

Johanna shivered. "Loesie, get on."

"Ghghghghghgh."

"Hurry up, we need to get out of here." What was going on with Loesie? Surely she wasn't afraid of a horse? The horses they'd use on the farm were big, too. She would know how to ride.

Loesie reached for the horse, but the moment she touched the reins, the animal stiffened. The ears went back. The head jerked up.

Roald said, "Whoa!"

Johanna's horse snorted and sidled sideways, also tossing its head.

"Calm down, calm down." She patted the horse's neck, but felt the muscles strain under the skin.

Loesie again reached out for the horse's reins. As she did so, the moonlight hit her bare hand, bathed in a silvery glow stronger than moonlight alone could have made it.

She yelled, "Wait."

Loesie's horse reared with a scream that echoed over the field. Loesie retreated, holding her arm over her head, away from the horse's kicking hooves.

Johanna's horse shied back. She had to hold on tightly just to stay on. Loesie's horse broke into a run around the other horses, its tail held high.

"Loesie, are you hurt?" Johanna reached out her hand to her friend. "Come over here." But her horse made unhappy noises and shied away from Loesie.

Roald slid off his horse. He made a grab for the reins of Loesie's horse, but it reared, kicking its front legs.

"Watch out!"

In the distance, the bandits' other horses replied. Some of them came running through the fields with a thudding of hooves. Men shouted in the village.

"Quick, get out. Hide." Johanna flicked the reins. Her horse took off with a speed she had thought impossible for a boring old packhorse.

CHAPTER 7

THE HORSE tore down a muddy path, throwing up clods of dirt with its hooves, and then plunged into the darkness of the forest. Johanna had to hold on with all her might not to fall off. The horse wouldn't stop. She had dropped the reins and they dangled somewhere down the sides of the horse's neck, but she couldn't get them without letting go of the edge of the saddle and if she did that, she would surely fall off. She had no idea if anyone still followed her. It was too dark between the trees. She thought she heard the sound of hooves behind her, but couldn't be certain. In fact, the further into the forest the horse went, the less certain she became.

A quick glance over her shoulder revealed only darkness. No sign of Roald's horse. No sign of the bandits. She had no idea where Nellie was, or whether Loesie had been left behind or had managed to climb on another horse. She had no idea and no control over where the horse was going. Only that it was going too fast. Distant voices echoed through the forest. Dogs barked. They would probably catch up soon. Or the bears would find her.

The horse ran and ran. Now they came through a section where it was darker than before, and where prickly branches slapped her sides. The horse's footfalls sounded muffled here. Trees grew close together here, forcing the horse into a trot and then a walk.

A scent of pine needles hung in the air.

Now that she no longer needed to hold on for life, Johanna fished up the reins which still dangled to the sides. The horse's flanks were wet with sweat. She pulled the reins.

"Whoa, stop."

The horse stopped, panting.

Johanna looked around. They were in a very dark spot between pine trees that grew so close that the tips of branches pricked through her dress.

Johanna listened.

The only sounds came from much further away: the rustling of leaves, the breaking of branches, the footfalls of hooves on the forest floor. No sounds that made it clear if these were bandits or her companions. No barking of dogs either.

Johanna waited, holding her breath to listen better. Whoever had been following her must also have stopped.

She let out her breath and held the next one.

Would Nellie, Roald and Loesie have been recaptured?

Poor Nellie.

What had Loesie done when touching the horse? She had ridden with the bandits for the past two days without much trouble. And then a chill: had she done it on purpose? She had done her best to help Loesie, but no one else had trusted her.

Where was Roald?

Her hand went to the ring she wore under her dress, which hung heavy against her skin. The key to keeping war out of Saardam and keeping the country together.

Johanna waited, but the sounds made by other people and horses faded until they were so faint that it was impossible to separate them from the sighing of the wind in the boughs.

Had they given up looking for her, sure that whatever lived in this forest would finish her off anyway?

She felt cold.

The trees whispered to each other in voices she couldn't hear. Animals scurried up there and talked to each other with little squeaks and squawks. They must be birds or the little long-tailed squirrels that ran up a tree trunk as if it was a horizontal path. Let's stay calm and not see things where there weren't any.

Johanna swung her leg over the horse and let herself slide to the ground. She landed in a carpet of pine needles that was soft and springy. The dense cover of pine trees made it so dark here that it was impossible to see the ground, but a bit further shafts of moonlight penetrated the canopy. The trunks of trees stood as silhouettes against the faint glow. They were strange trees, straight with dead branches at lower levels.

She tied the horse's reins onto a tree and peered between the foliage. The damp and cold air reached its fingers between the gaps in her clothes.

What would she do if no one from the group had escaped? Would making her own way through the forest be out of the question?

She should warn someone in Florisheim.

But you don't know where the bandits are going, the little voice that sounded like Nellie said.

But she knew some of their names, if they were real names.

Who in Florisheim is going to care about some foreign people when they probably have their own problems to deal with?

Nellie's voice was right. Alone, she couldn't do much,

never mind convince a foreign baron to send out men to look for a couple of girls, one of whom was a maid and the other bewitched, and a prince no one wanted to know about—all of them foreigners. Add to that the fact that she'd have to cross the duke's land first.

So she waited.

The biting cold made her shiver. She tried to keep herself warm by snuggling against the horse, but this particular horse was not the snuggling kind. It also refused to lie down and was probably more interested in finding a paddock than keeping a miserable human being warm.

Very slowly, morning light returned, first weak and blue, then brightening into the soft grey tones of mist. Johanna's view of the forest expanded with the increasing daylight. In places, the trees stood close to each other, but in other places light reached the forest floor and grass covered the ground. She could see no sign of anyone having passed this way.

Behind her, the horse pulled at the reins she had tied around a tree. Its ears twitched constantly.

What was it hearing? A wild animal? One of the bears? People?

Johanna held her breath and listened, but could make out nothing unusual over the sparse sounds of the forest. A bird chirped in a tree, not a kind she recognised.

Between the trees she noticed the outlines of a hill. Maybe if she climbed up there she would be able to see more.

She untied the horse, but no matter how she pulled the reins, the silly horse wouldn't move.

"Well then, have it your way." She retied the reins. The hill was not very far anyway. The horse could wait and mope here.

Johanna traversed the dense stand of pine trees, pushing low branches aside. The pine forest stopped suddenly and made way for beech trees.

Johanna climbed up the hill. It was bigger than the ancient burial mounds that they had seen yesterday. Much taller, too. As with the beech forest they had traversed, the ground cover consisted only of dead leaves. About halfway up the steep hillside, Johanna slipped in the moist leaves. She groped in the dirt to stop her slide down the hill, and her hands met a piece of wood buried sideways in the hillside. *As if it was a step.*

This hill had not been made by nature. Another burial mound?

When she got to the top, she found a slab of stone about a pace wide and two paces long set in the ground at the highest point of the hilltop. Slabs of stone came from quarries in Burovia or Westfalia. Johanna had seen places where stone came to the surface naturally, but that was further south in Lurezia. Not here. All building stone had to be carried downriver on barges like the *Lady Sara*.

That left the question: why was there a slab of stone in the middle of the forest?

She knelt and brushed away a cover of leaves.

Carved in the stone was a symbol that she didn't recognise. Two circles surrounded a head of an animal with large, hollow eyes. The mouth bore several pointed teeth. The head had a pair of cat-like ears, but the bottom jaw was missing from the image, either because the stone was age-worn or it had never been there. The carving looked like a skull.

Johanna reached out and her fingers touched the stone at the same time the little warning voice inside her said, *Stone magic!*

A deep chill went through her.

The grey dawn became night again. People screamed, primitive, beastly screams that were nothing like war cries. It was too dark to see, but even just the sounds made her sick. Gurgling death cries, screams of pain.

Johanna yanked her hand away from the stone, her heart thudding.

What sort of sorcery was this? She had no stone magic. Or had someone placed another trap of fear in this area?

She looked around her, but all she saw was trees and greenery, the greenness of the pine forest and the elegant trunks of the beech trees. Again, no sign of anyone having passed here recently. She slid down the hill, where she placed her hand on a beech trunk, but it only showed her tranquil forest. Apparently the pools of churned mud a bit further down were popular with a group of wild pigs. They had a whole bunch of striped piglets.

What sort of evil place had this been long ago?

She circled the hill. On the far side she noticed the narrow passage that led into the hill. It was not a hill, but a cool room or ice cellar of some sort. Or a treasure chamber.

Johanna glanced into the tunnel. Its walls were made from red bricks on either side, the brickwork arched at the ceiling. At the end of this passage, perhaps a few paces deep, was a door. It was a dark, featureless thing with a simple door handle and two latches, one at the top and one at the bottom.

A waft of chill air came from the passage. It was humid, but cold and laced with a tang of decay.

Johanna shivered. She had seen ice cellars in Burovia. She didn't like their rank wetness and the fact that one was here meant that a house or settlement couldn't be too far away.

That would be the duke's house and she wanted nothing to do with this duke.

She had better go back to the horse and get out of here. Find the river and then turn upstream. Beg the Baron to come with her. She *had* to find Roald.

Johanna started walking around the hill back to the stand of pine trees where she had left the stubborn horse, but at that moment, the barking of a dog echoed through the forest. And the gallop of a horse.

The bandits. She had to hide, quickly.

The beech trees surrounding the cellar offered no hiding places at all. There was only one hiding place short of running back to the pine forest.

In that dreadful tunnel.

Johanna pressed herself against the door at the back of the tunnel. The air here was cold and humid, and chilled her deep inside. The scent of cold wetness made her gag.

Through the tunnel entrance, she saw the bottom half of a horse pass close by. The animal's coat was brown, not black. She didn't recognise the boots of the rider.

The duke's men. If she didn't find a better hiding place, they would find her.

Johanna tested the door at her back. To her surprise, it opened.

A foul, cold waft came out. Urgh. She held her nose, inching further into the darkness. Outside, the sound of galloping hooves faded. Someone shouted, but it sounded far off and she couldn't hear the words.

While she listened, her eyes became better used to the darkness.

Blocks of ice were piled in huge stone basins that stood around the walls. Each basin had drainage holes in the bottom, from which melted water seeped into the earth, hence the smell.

Just an ice cellar. Winters weren't that cold in Saardam most years, and people in the city didn't have the luxury of cellars. They built cool rooms with thick walls. Having ice in summer was a luxury that was limited to years when winter was cold enough.

She tried to calm herself. There was nothing to worry about.

But the duke's men would find the horse and see that it was tied up. They would come and look for its rider

She had to find a better hiding spot. Johanna looked around. It was cold in here and the ground around those basins was wet. Some chunks of ice were really big and others had odd shapes like . . .

Hands?

Feet?

White-skinned, waxy. Open staring eyes. Wet hair, hollow cheeks. Naked breasts and buttocks.

CHAPTER 8

JOHANNA STAGGERED back towards the cellar's door.

Now that she knew what she was looking at, she counted at least half a dozen people kept frozen amongst large blocks of ice, some slowly leaking water on the stone floor. Now she really understood where the bad smell came from. Those were just the bodies she could see. It was too dark in the cellar to count the basins and who knew how many bodies were stacked up in each basin?

She heard the farmer girl Lenie's voice *People who go into the forest don't come back.*

Her head reeled.

Slowly, she backed out of the cellar into the tunnel. In between being stuck with dead people in here and live people outside, she took her chances with the live ones.

She closed the door firmly behind her and pressed herself in the little alcove in which the door was set. The cold air that seeped through the stone still carried the cloying scent of rankness. Her muscles shivered uncontrollably and she couldn't stop her teeth chattering.

It had become fully light outside. The mist had become thin enough for pink-tinged sunlight to skirt the tops of the trees.

The forest was full of sounds of horses' hooves and shouting men.

They would have discovered the horse by now. She should have let it loose. Johanna listened, but heard no screams from Nellie or anyone.

Maybe if she stood here very quietly, they would not find her. Surely, the person who kept dead bodies on ice would not want other people to know about this. The bandits wouldn't know that this cellar was here.

It was silly coming out here, because she would be safer inside, but she wasn't going to—

Someone came from around the back of the hill and looked in the tunnel. A guard in unfamiliar green and grey livery. He looked neat, with short-cropped hair and a short beard.

For a moment he froze, surprised. He and Johanna looked at each other. Before Johanna could run, he jumped forward and grabbed her by the arm.

Something clicked in Johanna's mind. In a time that seemed ages ago and a world away, she had heard a male voice tell her, *You hold their other arm and then twist. You have to do it quickly so you take them by surprise.* Johanna grabbed the soldier's wrist and twisted the arm that held her. To her surprise, her arm came free.

She ran. First down the hill, to gain speed.

The man's footsteps thudded behind her. He was so close, he would reach her in a moment. She expected the hand on her shoulder any moment. She swerved sideways through a field of bracken. He hadn't expected that. Sticks pulled at her dress. There was movement in the corner of her vision but she didn't see what or who it was. She ran.

Footsteps again thudded behind her, more than one person this time.

Someone whistled hard.

Johanna came into a clearing and there she faced two snarling bears. She screamed and turned around, but the soldier was close behind her.

One of the bears jumped. Johanna let herself fall in the leaf litter. She covered her head with her arms and ducked. Any moment now and its teeth would grab her by the throat or rip her head from her body. Someone shouted.

Silence.

Johanna waited.

Somewhere close by several people breathed hard. A bear snorted its hot breath into her neck.

"Get up," a harsh male voice said.

It was Sylvan, his face hard with anger. Behind him stood the duke's soldier. The two bears had been the ones that belonged to the bandits.

Johanna clambered to her feet, looking from one to the other. Her heart thudded like crazy against her ribs. Why was the duke's soldier with the bandits?

Sigvald came from behind and tied her arms behind her back. Sylvan watched with his brooding, angry expression. He held his arms folded over his chest.

Sigvald gave him an order, but Sylvan didn't move, and continued to glare instead.

Sigvald finished tying Johanna up. The rope drew tight around her wrists. He pushed her to the soldier, and said something that sounded like, "Take her to the others."

The soldier grabbed Johanna around the upper arm in a bruising grip. His fingers dug deep into the soft skin under her arms.

She protested. "Hey, ow! I can walk myself, you know?"

While the man continued dragging Johanna away, Sigvald stepped towards Sylvan, his hands planted at his waist.

He said something about orders.

"Fuck orders," Sylvan said. "We take all of them."

Johanna's captor stopped and looked over his shoulder.

"Who is the boss here?" Sigvald said.

Sylvan stuck his nose in the air. "No one who doesn't deserve to be."

"Say that again if you dare."

"I will. If you go back on your agreement, the men will distrust you and abandon you."

"And they'll trust you with your filthy magic?"

"Honest deeds go rewarded, always. Foul deeds breed distrust. I know that you've had no trouble—"

Sigvald swung his fist at him, but that was followed by a deep growl and a crack of branches. Both bears had jumped forward and faced Sigvald, poised to attack.

He retreated, his face red.

"Don't think I've forgotten this. I will not forget this, until I get the chance to put my sword through your arrogant heart."

"Dare try it."

There was a tense silence, and then Sigvald whirled around and stomped off to his horse.

The soldier pulled Johanna with him to a place where a group of people and horses had gathered.

Seated on the pine needle-covered ground, their hands tied like Johanna's, were Nellie and Roald. The soldier shoved Johanna down with them. Johanna's first thought was one of relief. The second thought . . .

"Where is Loesie?"

Nellie glanced to the side. Her left cheek showed a red mark in the shape of a man's hand. There was a bead of blood in the corner of her mouth.

Over the back of a horse hung a bundle in black clothing, which Johanna recognised as Loesie's dress. Her hair, dirty and knotted, hung down the horse's flank. Her hands dangled free, the fingernails broken and bloodied. Her heart jumped.

"Is she . . ."

"They gave her a good knock on the head, but she moves."

"She spooked the horses," Roald said. "That's why the thugs woke up."

Johanna nodded. The question remained whether Loesie did it on purpose or under the order of a master.

A couple of bandits joined the group leading the packhorses.

Their regular riding companions lifted Johanna, Roald and Nellie to their mounts. Roald managed to sit up straight even though his hands were tied, but Nellie slumped. Her cheek was growing purple.

The column set in motion, at a slow pace. Sigvald went in the lead.

Sylvan rode to the right-hand side, making his own path in the forest. The duke's man followed him, and the two bears and the hounds loped behind them. Occasionally he glared at the main party. Sigvald would spit in his direction and then Sylvan would increase the pace until all the main party saw was his horse's backside.

They now rode on clear paths, and the horses could go two or three abreast.

When Ludo's horse and Nellie's bandit's came next to each other, Johanna raised her hand to her face to indicate Nellie's swollen cheek.

"Does it still hurt?"

Nellie nodded. A tear ran over her cheek.

"Where did they catch you?"

"Not far from the house. The stupid horse turned back to

the village. The creep over there magicked the horse and it ran back to the others."

Next Johanna turned around to Roald, who was behind Nellie. His face looked pale and drawn. He didn't meet her eyes.

"How far did you get?"

He didn't reply.

Johanna remembered that first night when they had fished him out of the water and he hadn't spoken. He'd started banging his head into the wall.

"Please," she said softly. "Talk to me."

Roald continued to stare.

Nellie said, "He tried to protect me, but there were too many of them. That soldier man hit him real hard and then he screamed and he fell down. The bandits kicked dirt over him and laughed. He was frightened."

As frightened as he had been that first day when he went out in the hall and had to give a speech. Emotions didn't penetrate Roald's thoughts often, but she suspected that when they did, they made a profound difference.

Nellie's bandit kicked his horse into a trot so that it went to the lead of the column and out of earshot of Johanna.

Johanna met Roald's eyes. The look in his face disturbed her. "Hey, it will be all right. We're all still alive."

He said nothing. It was not all right.

She worried about what he had seen and what the bandits had done to Lenie, her brothers and her father. Hopefully, they hadn't blamed the family for their prisoners' escape.

So they rode on for the best part of the morning. Johanna had thought that the ice cellar had to be close to a house, and that the wide forest lanes with straight rows of trees on both sides indicated the same, but she had clearly been wrong, or this was a very large estate. Whatever the soldier was doing with the group, and when he had turned up, was a mystery to her, but he rode with Sylvan, constantly talking and joking. Whenever Ludo's horse came close enough for Johanna to hear their conversation, they discussed things that she wouldn't consider bandits' business: trade, a musical performance.

Sigvald glared at the pair of them.

He rode at the head of the main group, Sylvan at the other. Occasionally, the bears crossed the distance between the groups, but always ran back when Sylvan whistled.

The group startled a couple of deer, which jumped away with great elegant bounds. The hounds went after them, but they soon came back, panting, with their tongues hanging out of their mouths.

Some time after midday, the forest lane with its straight rows of trees opened out into a huge sun-drenched garden.

At the far end sunlight glistened off a lake with a large blocky house built from red clay bricks in the middle, on a small tongue of land. Green-painted shutters covered the windows, each with a stylised flower with alternating red and white petals in the middle. The garden was mostly ornamental, with neat hedges and flowerbeds in straight lines. There were roses and lavender bushes and other flowering plants which Johanna didn't recognise. The vegetable garden had been banished out of sight of the house, behind the stables. Johanna spotted bean stakes and cabbage.

The bandits dismounted at the edge of the garden. Sylvan and the soldier rejoined the group.

"We take them from here," Sylvan said.

Sigvald crossed his arms over his chest. He said something about payment that was not enough.

"You agreed to our terms. From the moment we captured them, you tried to talk me into doing what you wanted."

Sigvald said something about being stupid.

"I have my reasons. I can't help that you are incapable of following simple instructions. If it had been left up to you, they would have escaped."

Sigvald spat at Sylvan's feet. "You need me. You pay me. You don't pay enough, I take what belongs to me." He glanced at Nellie. Johanna didn't know how much she understood of this conversation, but her face was pale and drawn.

"Ha, none of them would fetch a good price. Every town on the river is flooded with people wanting work, even the kind of work no one wants to do. None of this lot are strong enough, or pretty enough, to interest people who can take their pick of hundreds of workers. You may *want* to sell them, but you can't."

Sigvald stared and didn't reply.

Sylvan stared back. Without breaking eye contact, he produced a pouch from his belt, which he tossed to Sigvald, who caught it in mid-air.

Sylvan said, "That's the last time I'll ever ask you to do a job."

"Fuck off, rich boy."

Sylvan balled his fist, but Sigvald had already turned his horse around. He whistled to his men.

"Bye, beauty." Ludo squeezed Johanna's backside and jumped from the back of the horse. The bandits riding with the other prisoners did the same.

They mounted the spare horses and with whistles and the flick of reins, the group left in gallop, leaving Sylvan and the soldier with the two bears and the four prisoners all on the biggest of the bandit's horses. Of course these animals did not belong to Sigvald and his group.

"Untie them," Sylvan said.

The soldier went to Roald first.

"Can you tell us what's going on?" Johanna asked.

"It will be my pleasure, lady, and I do apologise for your earlier treatment."

Having untied Roald, the soldier came to Johanna and used a dagger to slice through the rope. She flexed her wrists when the rope was off. The soldier helped her dismount and then went to help Nellie. Loesie had woken up. She didn't want to be helped, but was a competent enough rider to let herself down without accidents.

The horses stood passive, their heads lowered. One was trying to nibble on a bush, oblivious that a bear nosed around in the garden bed facing it.

Sylvan whistled. Furry heads went up, tails wagged and ears went forward.

"Get Karl to look after the animals," Sylvan said to the soldier.

"Certainly, sir."

The man took the horses' reins and led them up a path to the stables on the right of the garden. Hooves crunched on gravel. The dogs and bears followed meekly.

"I get in trouble when they destroy my father's roses," Sylvan said, while leading the group to the house.

His father? The duke?

Had he come to the river especially to capture the last of the Carmine House to take the group back to his father?

They arrived at a large gravel area in front of the castle's forbidding entrance. A broad set of steps led to the main doors, tall and painted green. Although there was no gate, the steps were the only connection to the castle across the land bridge, and Johanna imagined that those doors were very heavy and reinforced with iron bars.

A couple of swans swam peacefully across the water, followed by three fluffy grey cygnets.

"Look," Roald said, pointing. "Cygnets. Like Cygna."

His mother, the pale swan-like princess from the north.

The door to the castle opened with a mournful squeak and a thin man shuffled onto the forecourt. He was dressed in dark colours and wore his hair in a dark ponytail.

"There you are, master. Your father was expecting you back yesterday."

"We got delayed." Sylvan climbed up the steps and spoke to the man briefly. After a few words, the man went to the door, and Sylvan gestured for the others to come.

"Meet my father and enjoy the hospitality of the Swandale estate."

Johanna's mind still reeled from the turn of events. What was she supposed to think of this development? What kind of "hospitality" included guests that were brought in as prisoners?

The main entrance hall was a grandiose affair, with marble flooring, a grand staircase and an enormous chandelier. Giant oil paintings depicting severe-looking men with ruffled collars hung on the walls. They were quality paintings, too, looking so life-like that Johanna had to check several times to make sure that the men's gazes weren't following her.

It was quite dark here. The windows were small, and the walls were covered in dark green wallpaper. The few candles that burned in the chandelier didn't dispel a stuffy atmosphere.

The man led the group through the hall into a large room full of clutter: chairs, tables, few of them matching, shelves, book cases full of old works.

In a big armchair by the window sat a man. He was thin, in a well-worn house coat and matching slippers. A walking stick rested against the arm of his chair. He had a grey beard, clipped short, and a ring of hair surrounding his head. The top was bald and shone like a polished stone.

Apart from the fact that he was of the right age, he didn't look one bit like Baron Uti. In fact, he looked stern, but in a friendly way.

"Meet my father, Duke Lothar."

Johanna felt compelled to bow. Nellie did the same, but Roald stared at the duke, his brow furrowed. Did he recognise this man?

Loesie's gaze wandered off to the corner of the room, towards a cabinet with doors that held tiny panes of glass. Her irises had gone cloudy again. *Please, Loesie, behave yourself and stay out of trouble.*

"Father, these are the refugees I told you about."

Nothing about names. The bandits had never asked any of them for their names either.

"Hmph." The duke grabbed his walking stick. With a groan he heaved himself to his feet. Johanna was surprised how tall he was. Like father, like son. He shuffled to the group, looking Johanna in the eye.

"Some are magic-touched," Sylvan said.

"Is that true, hmmm?" The duke walked around the four of them.

From close up, his face was red and pore-riddled. His dark hair hung in greasy strings over the collar of his shirt.

His grey eyes met Johanna's in a flat look. She feared he would sense her magic, but he said nothing and his face remained blank. Then he went to Roald, who looked back at him as if he was a startled rabbit.

"This one's funny."

Sylvan said, "Don't worry about that one. He has as much magic as a farm dog."

The duke stopped at Loesie. "Ah, I see."

"Ghghghghgh!" Loesie retreated, but backed into a couch and fell backwards over the armrest onto the seat.

While Johanna called, "Loesie!" the duke grabbed Loesie's

shoulder. The chill of magic spread through the room. Loesie stiffened, her head thrown back.

"Loesie!" Johanna called.

"Be quiet, child," the duke snapped.

He bent over Loesie's prone form and pulled at her eyelid. She spat at him. Her eyes had clouded over to a luminous white.

"Hmmm, possession. That's interesting. I haven't seen any of those for a while." He chuckled, rubbing his hands. "Well, we might be able to fix that."

Johanna shivered. She wasn't sure if she wanted the man who kept dead bodies on his land to do anything to her friend.

He turned to Johanna. "Do any of you know who did this?"

How about: *You?* "We don't. She can't tell anyone. She can't talk."

"I presume she cannot write?"

"No."

Sylvan came to stand next to his father. "The person who has done this is someone strong enough to break open substream layers and infuse his own. He would have needed to win her trust to let him come close enough to do that. It's probably someone from her local area, someone she knows."

Substream layers?

His father turned to him. "Can't. There aren't any powerful magicians in Saarland. I know a few who could do that, but none who would bother with a Saarlander farm girl."

"Unless she was witness to something the magician did not want her to talk about."

Johanna saw Loesie hold the basket out to her. She remembered the images she'd seen when taking the basket— of men crossing the river and a woman's screams.

He was right: Loesie *had* seen something, and not wanting

her to talk was why the magician had shut her up. But what was it that she had seen? None of those nightly images were clear enough for Johanna to see much, or identify the attackers.

"This case is interesting, though." The duke stood back, rubbing his chin. "It seems that she has a certain level of innate magic that has clashed with the spell."

"I was wondering about that." Sylvan glanced at Johanna. She feared he was about to say, *That one has magic, too,* but he didn't.

The duke clapped his hands together. "Well, let's not treat them as criminals. They are tired and dirty. You are welcome to share dinner with us. We will try to solve this interesting situation in the morning. Hans!"

CHAPTER 9

THE SAME thin man who had opened the door for them now led the group back into the hall. In his prim-faced silence he preceded the group up the sweeping broad staircase into an upstairs corridor.

The walls were dark red here, and the doors a very dark brown. The ceilings had been painted white, but the paint had yellowed with age. The only light came from a tiny window at the very end of the passage and the light that fell in was dusky and didn't do much to dispel the closed-up, stifling atmosphere.

"Phooey, this place could do with an airing," Nellie said under her breath. Johanna agreed. Apart from the musty smell, the runner looked dusty, as if no one had walked through this corridor for ages.

How many people lived in this giant house?

They passed an open door to a room that was empty, except for a carpet and floor-length heavy drapes that half-covered the window. The small panes of glass were dirty on the outside and spiders had built webs in the corners of the window frame.

"Does only the duke's family live in this house?" Johanna asked, but the stiff servant didn't reply.

He opened a door to the left. Inside, dark curtains hung before the window, almost blocking daylight. There were three beds with dark frames and velvet bedspreads. A chair that had seen better times sat in front of an empty fireplace. A cupboard against the side wall held a variety of handmade dolls. It looked like this had been a children's room.

"Two can sleep here," the servant named Hans said in a clipped, heavily accented voice.

The next room was larger and had a double bed, a hearth and a couple of chairs. The walls were dark red.

"Sleep in this room or this room," the servant said. "I bring water for washing."

The man took them to third room where every bit of wall space that had no window or door was taken up by wardrobes, all of them filled with clothes. Men's, women's, in a variety of styles, but most a bit old-fashioned.

Hans said in his clipped voice, "Wash. Find clothes. Come to dinner. Downstairs." He bowed, turned around and left the group to stand awkwardly in the hallway.

Well, what to do?

Loesie had turned around and was studying a portrait that hung on the wall, depicting a man in a ruffled shirt wearing a hunter's hat. His face vaguely resembled the duke's.

"You and Roald must sleep in this room," Nellie said, indicating the room with the double bed. "We will sleep in the other room." Coming from Nellie, who was petrified of Loesie, that meant a lot.

Johanna wasn't sure if she wanted to sleep in any room. Much as she appreciated a real bed or being free of Ludo's leery stares, she didn't want to be fooled into thinking that they were visitors here.

"I'd rather have all of us in the same room. I'm afraid I

don't trust anyone here." *And I don't trust Loesie.* If she was the reason Sylvan had brought them here, he must know more about her than he let on.

"No, Mistress Johanna, you must be with your husband."

Get on with producing an heir.

Johanna resisted the urge to roll her eyes. How quickly Nellie had recovered from the ride through the forest. Dependable, unflappable Nellie.

Instead of arguing about who was going to sleep where, Johanna went into the third room, with all those wardrobes against all the walls. Nellie opened the door to one of them. It was full of dresses, mostly heavy dark velvet ones of the type that Johanna had tried on with Mistress Daphne but had found unsuitable for the ball. This type of dress, buttoned up to the neck with few frills, must be eastern fashion. She pulled one out and ran a hand over the fabric. It was very heavy and thick.

"Quite old-fashioned," Nellie said, hanging the dress back. She opened another door. Inside was a variety of men's clothing, some of the jackets visibly dusty at the shoulders.

"They are very pretty clothes," Roald said.

Nellie wrinkled her nose. "I don't like this one bit. Who else lives here? Why does he have all these clothes here?"

"For guests?" Roald said.

"Who would be travelling in this area? We've come through the sand. It's horrible. No one goes that way. There is no trade, no farming, nothing of importance out there, only trees."

Johanna couldn't help think of the bodies in the ice cellar. She didn't know whether to bring it up or whether this duke would have some sort of magic that allowed him to listen in on the conversations. Or whether the cellar was even on his land.

She pushed the uneasy thoughts away.

"I think these clothes have been here for a long time." Nellie said. "They're quite old-fashioned and could use an airing. But we better choose something. If we're to go to a formal dinner, we need to clean up. You two are the future of Saardam. You need to look the part."

"Nellie, they might have untied us, but we're still prisoners."

"That doesn't mean we lose our dignity."

"Dignity would mean not using this man's clothes."

"Go to a formal dinner in these?" Nellie spread her hands. Her dress had a tear down the front and was smudged with dirt. Roald had been wearing a farmer's vest, which was extremely dirty. Loesie had refused to change into anything new even after they collected clothes from the farm. She still wore her grandmother's black dress, now smudged with mud and other substances.

Johanna sighed. Yes. They could not attend a formal dinner in their own clothes, and there really was no other option but to use the duke's.

They found a blue dress for Johanna and a ruffled shirt and green velvet jacket for Roald. The two of them went into the room with the double bed, where Hans had brought the promised water and cloths. Johanna draped the clothes on the bed and proceeded to take off Roald's filthy garments.

"I should shave. Do you know how to do that?"

Johanna dipped cloth into the basin and wrung it out. "I think a beard looks fine on you, if you can keep the food out of it." She scrubbed his chin, where flecks of white stuff had dried in the stubble

"I know how to eat properly, if we get tableware."

She had no doubt that he did.

"Do you think that I can look at you tonight?" He stood with his arms wide while she dipped the cloth in the water again.

"Is that the only thing you ever think about?"

"No, but I like looking at you. Take that dress off." He reached for her bodice.

She batted his hand away. "Not now. We're supposed to be at dinner with the duke. Do you know the duke?"

"I told you about him. He tried to kill his half-brother several times."

"Yes, I remember you telling us, but have you met him before?"

"He would have recognised me if we met."

True. She washed his neck and chest, his arms—

"Take off that dress. I want to see you."

"I think you need a little cooling down." She thrust the cloth into his crotch, where his member stood up like a crooked stick.

"That's cold!" He tried to push her away.

She tickled his side and he burst out giggling. "Heeee, don't do that. Don't do that!"

They fell in a heap onto the bed and rolled over the cover, scattering pillows.

Someone knocked on the door. "Are you all right, Mistress Johanna?"

"Yes, Nellie, don't worry." She met Roald's eyes. He managed to look surprised.

"You're silly," she said. Silly, inappropriate, but funny. He trusted her. He needed someone to tell him what to do, and he listened to her.

She pushed herself up from the bed. "Come, let's put on these horrible clothes."

She helped him into shirt and trousers, quickly washed herself and wormed herself into the dress. She asked Roald to do up her laces at the back, but he didn't seem to know how to, so she had to ask Nellie.

Roald stopped her when she went out the door. "I love

you. I haven't said it yet today." His face was humourless and sincere. She knew he was only repeating what his mother had said to him, and he didn't understand love. But he understood being safe and comfortable.

She stroked his stubbly cheek. His grey eyes met hers in their usual sincere look. "You love me, too?"

"Yes. Yes, I think so."

He smiled, really smiled, while his eyes met hers. A cheeky smile that spoke of silly, naughty and slightly inappropriate things. She had never seen him smile like this and had thought he was incapable. It was beautiful and filled her with hope. They would find safety, they would return to Saardam, they would defeat the occupiers, they would rebuild the city, they would have a big family with lots of little chubby babies.

Tears sprang to her eyes.

"You're crying."

"Because . . . because I think that we can get out of here safely and go back home, and there will be a home to fight for."

She wasn't sure that he understood, but that didn't matter.

She kissed him fleetingly on the lips before going out the door.

In the wardrobe room, she found Nellie going through the dresses and Loesie standing in front of the window. Nellie made every effort not to look at Loesie, and Loesie had her arms crossed over her chest.

"I told her that she needs to change out of that filthy dress, mistress, but she just makes filthy noises at me."

Loesie said, "Ghghghghghgh!" She turned back to the window.

Something in the tone of her voice made Johanna feel cold. The duke sensed her magic. He said there was something odd going on with Loesie, that her own magic had clashed with the magic of the person who had tried to put a spell on her. Did she believe him, that he wasn't that person?

"Yes, well, let's worry about you first, Nellie."

She asked Nellie to do up the back of her dress and then went through the wardrobes in search of a dress for Nellie to wear.

Nellie was both embarrassed and delighted to choose.

"These clothes are much too nice for me. I'm only a maid."

"When we get back to Saardam, you'll have to wear much nicer dresses than this one."

"How so, Mistress Johanna?"

"You don't think I'm going to leave you behind? If I move into the palace, you'll come. You can be my Lady-in-Waiting."

Nellie's eyes widened. "Really?"

"Yes, Really." Nellie was not, and had never been, "only a maid". Then Johanna had an odd thought. Her own ambitions had been to run the Brouwer Company. What about Nellie's ambitions? Maybe they were intertwined with hers. Unable to work for herself, with an unsupportive and religious family, Nellie's future depended on Johanna's.

Nellie had chosen a dark red dress that looked too severe on her.

"I don't like that dress. It makes you look old."

"I agree. It's not the kind of thing I should be wearing. These clothes are all so expensive—"

"Cowpats, Nellie. The duke wants a dress-up party with pretty young girls. He doesn't care about who you are or who I am. I don't even know if he's got any maids himself or if that sour man is the only other person in the house."

"Don't forget the son. He's quite handsome."

"Handsome?" With all the will in the world, she couldn't call Sylvan and his tattoos and ugly scar handsome. "Don't you feel his magic?"

Nellie frowned. "Magic?"

"He's a dark magician. He may be young or handsome to you, but don't underestimate him. He's dangerous."

Nellie had to settle for the red dress, because there wasn't anything more modern that would fit her slender frame. Johanna combed out Nellie's hair. It was full of knots, but she managed to do it up in a bun. A brooch and necklace completed the ensemble.

Nellie stood in front of the mirrored glass, twisting and turning this way and that.

"You look good, Nellie, stop worrying."

"I'm not sure, Mistress Johanna. What about . . ." Her gaze went to the bonnet that she had left on the arm of a chair.

"No, it's filthy."

Nellie didn't protest, but continued to look at her reflection, as if checking that it was really her.

Now it was Loesie's turn. She stood in front of the window, looking into the garden. Pale light fell on her face.

Johanna took two dresses from the cupboard that looked like they might fit and were of the dour and black type that Loesie favoured. One had no lace at all, but the other had a little bit, and might look quite good.

Then she called, "Loesie?"

She turned around. Her eyes were wide, but no longer clouded over. Johanna wondered if that only happened when there was strong magic in the air.

"We need to get you dressed for dinner."

"Gghghghghgh!" She shook her head so violently that her hair danced around her head.

"Why, what's wrong?" Nellie said. "Look, Mistress Johanna has even chosen a dress for you that looks like that horrible thing you're wearing now used to, before it got so disgusting. Why don't you for once do what she says? You know that she's—"

"Never mind, Nellie." She probably had been about to say that Johanna was the princess now, but that should remain unsaid. There was yet no evidence that the duke knew who Roald was.

Johanna held up the dress with the lace. "See, this one is not so bad—"

"Ghghghghghghgh!" Loesie backed away.

"What's going on, Loesie? It's only a dress. You can't go to a dinner with a duke looking like this."

"Hmmmmmm!"

"You don't want to come?"

Loesie shook her head.

"If you don't want to go to dinner, then what are you going to eat?"

Loesie shrugged.

"Well, you may not care but I do. Try this dress on." She undid the laces at the back.

But Loesie's behaviour made Johanna feel uneasy.

Johanna didn't like any of these clothes and the reason they might be here any better than Loesie did, but the fact was, she had no evidence whatsoever that the duke even knew about the dead people in the ice cellar, or that the cellar was on his land. These clothes might be here legitimately. They were old enough to have belonged to old family members who once lived here and died—

More dead bodies. She shuddered.

She whispered close to Loesie's ear, "Is the duke the person who put this spell on you?"

Loesie shook her head again.

"You're afraid of him?"

Loesie nodded. She made some hand signs that Johanna didn't understand.

Whatever magic had passed between them when the duke examined Loesie downstairs had been strong enough that Johanna could feel it.

"We're all afraid. We can't let them find out who we are. We must make it look like we're just ordinary travellers. Please, put it on, Loesie."

Johanna pulled Loesie's black dress over her head. The fabric felt greasy to the touch, and it smelled terrible. Loesie's underclothes weren't much better, so she had to find a clean chemise and drawers. Loesie's skin was pale and reminded Johanna uncomfortably of bodies, except the near-translucent skin showed blue veins underneath. Her ribs stuck out, and her stomach was hollow.

It was eerie, really. "You're much too thin, Loesie."

She helped Loesie into the dress. It turned out to be dark green instead of black. Nellie fussed over the colour, because Roald also wore green and Johanna should wear the same colour—

"Nellie, it's a game the duke wants to play with us. We're not guests and it isn't the royal ball."

"Just making sure he doesn't get any wrong impressions about who belongs with who. . . ."

"Ghghghgh!" Loesie hissed at her.

Johanna said, "Stand still. How am I supposed to do up your corset if you keep moving?"

Wasn't tonight going to be fun with those two sleeping in the same room?

Roald had come into the room and waited patiently at the door. He looked surprisingly regal in the green jacket and shirt with ruffles.

Finally they were all done and ready for playing dress-ups with a mass-murderer.

B Y NOW the light outside had faded to deep orange and the gloomy hallway had become even darker. Johanna walked first, followed by Nellie and Roald with Loesie bringing up the rear.

In the huge entrance hall, their footsteps echoed against the ceiling. The huge crystal chandelier hung on a chain suspended on a pulley mechanism, so that the household staff could light the few candles up there. The ceiling was painted in dark colours with scenes depicting destruction and a man pointing towards a light.

"Who is that?" Nellie whispered to Johanna, because talking aloud didn't seem appropriate in the intense silence.

"It's the True God from the Belaman Church, I think."

"I thought the Belaman Church was even stricter on magic than the Church of the Triune."

"The fact that the duke's ceiling bears religious scenes doesn't mean that he adheres to the teachings."

Nellie swallowed visibly.

The Belaman Church had many branches, and the Church of the Triune was sometimes considered part of it, but their stance against magic united them all. Instead of believing in the Lord of Fire, they believed in Doom. It was a place without leader, a place where voices were not heard because there was no sound.

In fact, she imagined Doom to be a bit like this hall: abandoned and dusty.

When coming in, she had not noticed the draughtiness of the hall and the dust on the chandelier. Candle wax had dripped onto the stairs in several places, and it was blackened and worn with people having walked across it for some time.

The house was quiet except for a few chinks of porcelain that had to come from the kitchen.

They found the dining room through a door under the stairs. Inside stood a long table with a dark blue velvet cover, gold-rimmed plates and crystal glasses. There were two standing chandeliers, and a lusty fire burned in the hearth. Since it had now started to go dark outside, the drapes were closed, and the room was bathed in a warm yellow glow.

The duke sat at the head of the table. He had changed into a velvet coat which was a rather garish dark purple, and the shirt he wore underneath was excessively ruffled. He indicated the other chairs with an exaggerated gesture of his hand.

"Sit down, friends."

Johanna battled the impulse to say *We're not your friends*, but she didn't. No doubt this man was using his henchmen or his magic to keep his "guests" here.

Sylvan came out of the shadows and took his place at the other end of the table. He had changed into an equally severe blue jacket that made him look more brooding.

Johanna eyed him. *Handsome?* Seriously?

They sat down, Johanna and Roald on one side of the table, Nellie and Loesie on the other.

The duke asked for a moment's silence. "True God, we

pray that our weary travellers may enjoy our meagre hospitality and that they may continue their journey safely."

Johanna was getting very irritated with these people's insistence on ignoring the fact that they had been captured.

Nellie was eying Sylvan.

Loesie looked oddly elegant in the dress, and her thin arms and long, spider-like fingers gave her an ethereal presence. Her hair was darker than that of typical Saarlanders. Johanna remembered Loesie telling her that she had only a mother on the farm. Who was her father? She had never given it much thought. Loesie had told her once that he had died of illness while working at a neighbour's farm. Johanna had never considered that he might have been a foreign guest worker, or even that her mother and father might never have been married. He had probably been Estlander, because there was only one thing that Saarlanders with magic abilities had in common: eastern blood.

A dour-faced woman came in and brought a tray with a silver lid which she placed in the middle of the table. The thin man brought several gold-rimmed terrines with cooked vegetables.

"Time to have the cook's specialty," the duke said. "Roast venison from the forest."

Johanna shivered, thinking of the ice cellar.

They were silent while Hans came forward and took the lid off the tray. He cut a piece which he offered to the duke who tasted it and nodded his approval.

Then he proceeded to carve the meat, doling out steaming portions to all around the table. It smelled heavenly.

Then he poured something that looked like cider.

In Saardam, only the church used wine, and then not much of it. Grapes grew on hillsides further to the south.

When they finished serving, the maid and Hans retreated. The duke lifted his glass. "We drink to this memorable occasion." The candlelight made deep shadows over his old face.

What was so memorable about being a prisoner here, Johanna didn't know.

Roald lifted his glass in turn. "To this occasion." He took a sip of the cider and set the glass on the table. His face remained blank. Someone must have spent a lot of time drilling him in these exchanges.

She thought of the unguarded smile on his face when they were cavorting over the bed in the room upstairs. The man who hid behind this impersonal mask was not dumb at all. Just very, very awkward.

Nellie sat straight-backed, staring at Loesie, who was trying to work out in which hand to hold the spoon.

Johanna could no longer contain her desire for answers. "Can I ask what your interest is in us?"

"Is it improper to offer a meal and a dry bed to travellers?"

"We're not travellers. Those men captured us. We were minding our own business and they took us from our ship." He glared at Sylvan, who glared back at her.

"My men found you wandering on our land."

"We were in an orchard along the river. Do you have land that far away from here?"

"I do."

"Do you do the same to all river traders who stop off?"

"True river traders keep going. They don't stop off at places where no people live."

True.

"We are not river traders. We're refugees with no place to go."

She gave Loesie a sideways glance. Isolated as this estate was, did he know about the devastation of Saardam and Aroden? If he treated all his visitors to a meal, people might have told him in this room.

She put down her spoon and carefully wormed her hand under the table. The moment her fingertips contacted the wooden underside of the table, a rush of cold went through her. Images flowed unbidden through her mind: a fire-lit sky, someone jumping off the quay, Roald, wet and pale, in the cabin of the *Lady Sara*, the skulls and bones in the ash of the burnt farm, the children yelling at the *Lady Sara* at Aroden, Roald looking at her. Somewhere in the background, Nellie prompted, "Say: I do."

And he said, "I do," and slid his ring over Johanna's finger, where it dangled loose because it was much too big.

Johanna gasped and withdrew her hand.

What in all of heaven's name was this? She stared at her plate, her heart thudding. She had expected the wood to show her things, not invoke her own memories. Wait—did that mean the wood sucked out her memories? Did that mean the duke would now know for certain who they were— if he didn't know already?

The duke had asked Nellie a question. She was stammering something about a farm and selling baskets and cheese. Presumably the question had been about Loesie.

Then another thought: not since they had set foot in his house had the duke asked for their names.

That's because he already knows.

"And what is your relationship to this strange possessed girl?" the duke asked.

"I . . . um," Nellie said, and met Johanna's eyes in a kind of *help me out* look.

"She is my friend," Johanna said.

"It's very odd for a daughter of a rich merchant to have a friend who comes from a farm."

So he knew her father. Well, he might have recognised the *Lady Sara*.

"Yes, well, my mother is no longer alive as you might

know, and I help my father, so I go to the markets to buy and sell things. That's where I've met her."

"Hmm, is that so?" He stroked his beard. "Could it also be that both of you share a certain ability?"

"What do you mean?" She was trying to sound as innocent as possible.

"You know very well what I mean. Magic is rare in Saarlanders."

"It is not so rare amongst the river traders."

"Ha, most of them are peddlers. They buy small trinkets: talismans or mistwood. They may have a tiny bit of magic and the wood shows them things. Then they fancy themselves magicians. Ha!"

He put a piece of meat in his mouth.

"Both of you are different. My son says that he could feel your magic quite strongly."

Sylvan nodded.

"Is that a reason to take us prisoner?"

He had been cutting his meat and put knife down. "You do not know anything about magic, do you, child?"

She wanted to say, *I'm not a child, I'm a married woman,* but didn't. Her heart was thudding against her ribs.

"I guess I can't blame you, coming from that ignorant place, full of priests who live in constant denial of what they could see before their very eyes if only they opened them."

Roald protested, "Hey, you don't call—"

"Shhh." Johanna put a hand on his arm, careful not to touch the table.

"Yes, tell him to be quiet. Keep pretending that magic doesn't exist, and my half-brother will overrun the entire coastal plain. You don't believe that I brought you here for your protection, because you need to know about magic, and you need this situation . . ." He flapped his hand at Loesie. ". . . solved. She is leaking so much magic in the substream that all of us can feel her. That's why you're here. She will attract my half-brother. He will use her, and you have no idea what his court magicians can do."

"You mean Baron Uti?"

"The very one."

"But . . ." She remembered the baron in the party of guests walking into the hall with the royal family. She had not sensed any magic around him, but—wait. Court magicians. Kylian.

He had looked at her and picked her out of the crowd. He had tried to seduce her and then when the fire demons hit, he had vanished.

She met the grey eyes of the man who, according to Roald, had tried to kill his half-brother. And he honestly did not look like a killer. He might have tried because he considered his brother a danger to everyone. Or he might not. Even in business, the people who looked least likely to default on their payments sometimes did.

How could she know?

Do not get involved in this feud. It has nothing to do with Saardam.

Except it did, because of Loesie.

"You have brought us here because . . ." She licked her lips, finally putting some pieces of this strange situation together. "Are you an exorcist?"

The duke laughed. "They love words like that in the west, don't they, son?"

Sylvan flicked his eyebrows in a kind of "get on with it" gesture.

"Are you?"

"If that's the kind of answer you want and the kind of language you like to use, yes, I am." The look in his grey eyes was intense. He pushed his chair back, picked up the walking stick that leaned against the edge of the table next to him, and shuffled to a cabinet against the back wall. His stick went *tap, tap, tap* on the floor.

The cabinet was made from dark wood and had doors with small panes of glass through which Johanna couldn't see anything because of the reflection of the candles in the glass.

He fiddled about with a key and opened the door with a creak. From inside, he produced a cup, a signet ring and a gnarled and knotted piece of wood, which he placed on the table. The cup was an odd thing, made of dark glass and heavily decorated with gold paint.

The duke returned to the back wall, to another cupboard. *Tap, tap, tap.*

Next he brought a cage to the table. It was an ugly thing, made out of rusty iron, and big enough to fit a large cat. There was a little door at the front, which the duke opened by lifting a latch that seemed too heavy for a door of that size.

He went back to another cupboard.

Roald frowned at the cage. "What's that for?"

"That's for holding the demon, young man," the duke said, his back to them.

The servant Hans came in and quickly collected the plates and trays. Johanna noticed how he stayed well clear of the objects his master had put on the table.

Nellie met Johanna's eyes and frowned. "What's that for?" she mouthed.

Johanna shrugged.

Loesie glared at the duke's back, her face a mask of distrust.

The duke came back to the table, *tap, tap, tap*, and put a carafe next to the cup. He placed the walking stick so that it leant against the edge of the table and made a show of slowly lowering himself in the chair with a groan.

"What's all this for?" Johanna asked into the silence.

The duke waited until Hans had carried out the last tray of plates and tableware and shut the door behind him. He poured a dark fluid from the carafe into the cup.

"We must first determine the nature of your friend's possession," he said, swirling the fluid in the cup.

Johanna heard Reverend Romulus talk about goat's blood and black sorcery. That fluid didn't *look* like blood. It looked like very dark wine.

"Should some of us perhaps wait outside?"

Roald watched with an expression of intense interest, but Nellie's face had gone white as a ghost's.

The duke turned to her, surprised. "Why?"

"Because the possession concerns only my friend, and me. Perhaps."

Duke Lothar chuckled. "So, you're afraid, young lady?" He pointed the bit of gnarled wood at Nellie, who bent back, so that the wood didn't touch her. Her were wide. She nodded.

"She's got nothing to do with this," Johanna said.

"What about him?" He poked the wood at Roald, who didn't flinch and gave the knot of wood a cold stare, as if it were a dead fish.

Johanna's heart thudded. If the duke knew who Roald was, he sure did a good job of acting like he didn't. "He has nothing to do with the possession either. Let both of them go to their rooms."

Roald started, "No. I need to protect my—"

Johanna cut him off. "Yes, he's got nothing to do with this."

"All right." The duke leaned back. He seemed amused. "All right, let them go."

Nellie jumped to her feet as if she had been sitting on a spring. Roald didn't move. Johanna wanted to get up and bodily push him out the door. Every minute he remained in this room was one where his identity could be discovered.

But if she seemed too keen to have him gone, the duke *would* suspect something.

Nellie said, "Aren't you coming?"

Roald said, "No." And Johanna said, "Yes."

The duke pointed the wood at Roald again. "He's not afraid. She isn't afraid either." He pointed in the direction of Loesie, and Loesie batted the wood away—

Johanna shouted, "Don't touch it!"

But it was already too late. Magic flashed through the room.

Loesie stiffened. Her eyed widened and went luminous white. She opened her mouth and let out a bone-chilling wail.

Nellie screamed.

Sylvan yelled at her, "Shut up!"

While Loesie slowly fell face first onto the table.

"Loesie!" Johanna pushed her seat back so hard that the chair fell over. She rushed to her friend's side. Loesie's skin was ice cold.

"What have you done?" she screamed at the duke.

Loesie went, "Hmmmmm!" She pushed herself up, her eyes like shining slits of whiteness. She balled her hands into a knot, her fingers white-knuckled.

"Hmmmm! Ghghghghghgh!" She swayed from side to side. Her mouth moved but no sound came out.

"Talk to us," the duke said. "Talk to us, talk to us." In a chanting voice.

Nellie had remained by the door, the doorknob in her hand. Her face was so white that she might faint any moment.

More than anything, Johanna wanted to get Roald out of here. Whatever was going to happen, it wasn't going to be good.

In her mind, she heard the Reverend Romulus' voice talking about quackery and goat's blood. Rituals from the

Lord of Fire. Black magic. Necromancy. Dead bodies in the ice cellar.

"Talk to us, talk to us, talk to us."

Loesie gave an animal-like snort.

"It won't work like this." Even Sylvan's voice sounded concerned.

"Talk to us, talk to us, talk to us."

"Father, there is more going on than simple possession. This is not a spell cast by a peddler. You can't break it like this."

Loesie produced a low hum. Her face was tilted to the ceiling, her eyes luminous white, leaking wisps of mist. She swayed in her seat and the duke swayed in the same rhythm. Had his eyes always been so cloudy?

"Father!" Sylvan sprang forward, roughly shoving his father's chair around. The walking stick slid to the ground with a loud clatter. Sylvan nearly tripped over it. "Father!" He shook his father's shoulders.

The duke's eyes re-focused. "Huh, what?" He stared at his son, his expression confused. "What are we—" He looked around.

Loesie still sat swaying from side to side. Her hum made her chest vibrate. Johanna wanted to clamp her hands over her ears.

"Do something!" Nellie yelled.

Roald simply stared, his face in an expression of intense curiosity.

Still humming, Loesie picked up the goblet. Her hand trembled so much that the wine spilled over the sides, first onto the tablecloth, but then on her dress as she lifted it to her mouth. She drank. Wine flowed past the sides of the cup down her chin, down her neck, over her chest, leaving dark red trails.

She put the cup down and sat as if frozen, staring into nothingness.

"What's going on?" Johanna whispered when the silence lasted too long.

Sylvan pushed Loesie's shoulder, but there was no reaction. Her eyes blinked, but the irises still shone luminous white.

Then Loesie sprang up from her chair. With stiff steps, she staggered towards the window. Her hands shook visibly. Her eyes blinked fast. Her bottom lip trembled; even her hair seemed alive. She was shaking too much to keep walking. Johanna glanced at the duke or Sylvan, but they didn't look like they knew what to do either.

Nellie watched from near the door, covering her mouth with her hand.

And Loesie's shaking still increased, until the entire room seemed to be shaking with her. She held her hands out in front of her, her fingers curved like claws. Now even her breathing was coming in gasps.

Johanna couldn't stand it anymore. "Is someone going to do anything?"

Nellie yelled, "No, don't go near her!"

And Loesie let out an ear-splitting cry, that descended into a gasping gurgle, and a cough. She coughed and coughed, and leaned forward.

Johanna patted her on the back. A visible muscle spasm went through Loesie's body, and with a loud burp, a gush of dark vomit welled out of her mouth.

The mass hit the floor with a wet splash and spatters going everywhere. And another lot.

It was very dark-coloured because of the wine. Too dark, really, almost black. And it moved of its own.

Johanna backed away, wiping dark specks from her shoes.

Nellie screamed. "Oh, look! They're spiders!"

It was true. Thousands and thousands, millions of them, spreading out over the floor. Loesie coughed and vomited up more of them, covered in trails of slime. She coughed and vomited, struggling for breath. Gasping. Vomiting into her hands. Gasping.

She was going to faint.

Johanna stepped forward. She had to help her friend.

"No, wait." Sylvan pushed her roughly out of the way. With one hand he grabbed Loesie, who was about to collapse in her own spidery vomit. With his other hand, he made a sweeping gesture at the floor. He spoke a few harsh-sounding words.

A blast of cold air went through the room that blew out all the candles. The curtains whipped up. The fire flared in the hearth. The flames were blue.

Then silence returned.

The spidery mass had turned to water. Sylvan caught Loesie as she collapsed.

He carried her to a chair, her head lolling over his arm.

Then he re-lit the candles on the table. His hand didn't even shake.

"Hmmm?" Loesie said. She opened her eyes and pushed herself up. "Johanna?"

"Loesie!" Johanna was about to hug her friend, but Sylvan held her back.

"Wait. She's not completely cured."

Johanna retreated. The whiteness had gone from Loesie's eyes. "Can you say something to me?"

"What are we doing here?"

Sylvan was right. The voice was Loesie's, but the accent was not. Loesie spoke like a farm girl.

"She's a true witch," the duke said, leaning back in his chair. He wiped sweat from his forehead. His face had taken on an ashen grey tone. "I can't perform a full exorcism here. I will need to tap the magic lines."

Whatever that meant.

"We have to take her out into the forest."

Johanna's unease developed into full-blown panic. No, she did not want to go into that forest again. "We were on our way to town to find someone to cure her."

"You won't find anyone else. I can cure her, but I'll need a rest first. You will have to lift the curse from her before you reach Florisheim. I assume this is where you were travelling?"

Johanna gave him a suspicious look. "Haven't you heard what happened in Saardam?"

"Sadly, I have. A lot of people have come up the river and told us the tales. My own brother was there and managed to escape with his life. He's been back scarcely a day."

Curiosity took over. "You've spoken to him?" The man he was supposed to have wanted to kill. She didn't know that they were that close to the town.

"I have."

"Do you know how much of Saardam was burned? Who were the attackers? Who rules the city now?"

"Word goes that the fire was started by the members of that church of theirs and that they now—"

At the same time Nellie said, "Impossible." Johanna said, "Cowpats!"

And Nellie glared at her in a you-don't-use-that-language-in-presence-of-a-duke kind of way.

Johanna composed herself. "I don't believe that for one moment. A lot of people, especially the nobles, hate the church, but they would never do something like that. Also, they forbid magic, and the fire was started with magic."

"I'm merely repeating what many people have been saying. I can't verify the rumour without going there. The news is also that the church has instated a governor."

Johanna almost said *cowpats* a second time, but didn't think Nellie would survive that.

"Who is this governor of the church?" Next he was going to say *Reverend Romulus* and that would just show how much these rumours were worth—

"A man who calls himself Alexandre."

"Who?" She looked at Nellie. "Do you know him?"

Nellie shook her head. On Nellie's other side, Loesie sat frowning at the duke.

"According to refugees, this man has instated himself as regent. My brother isn't happy about it. If anything, his son could claim the throne if the Saardam royal family does not show up anywhere."

Johanna's heart thudded in her throat. Roald's ring hung heavy against her chest. "Has anyone seen where they went?"

"They fled like cowards."

They didn't.

Johanna met his grey eyes and returned his stare until she had to look away. If he expected her to say something about the royal family, he was going to be disappointed.

She didn't want to stay in this man's house or eat his food, or wear his clothes.

He put his hands on the armrests of his chair. "Go to bed now, my friends. Tomorrow, I will undertake the task of driving the remnants of the demon from your friend's soul, and then you can travel on. You *should* travel on. Many refugees have come from Saarland to Florisheim, and you will surely find people amongst them you know."

Father. Although she didn't dare hope.

CHAPTER 11

SYLVAN ACCOMPANIED the group back through the hall. They walked slowly, with Johanna and Sylvan supporting Loesie between them. She could walk but wasn't very steady on her feet. She kept asking how they got here, and no matter how many times Johanna explained, the answer didn't stick. The voice was Loesie's, but the accent too cultured to belong to her.

Going up the stairs was a struggle, with Loesie unable to lift her feet far enough, and the effort it required rendered her silent.

Johanna's eyes met Sylvan's. "I find it had to believe that your father lets us go so easily."

"Do you? He is only interested in the magical. He's not interested in you, just in the demon. He's wanted to capture a demon for a while."

"And then do what with it?" She thought about the rusty cage on the table.

"My father likes to invent things. It is his dream to make a *machine* powered by magic. He wants a magical creature so that he can force it to lend its essence to moving the machine."

"Does he perform magic a lot?" *Like, try to bring people back from the dead?* Treading into dangerous territory now.

"He likes to. I have to hold him back sometimes. He thinks he's better than he is."

"It sounds dangerous."

"To him, yes. To everyone else, not so much. We're on an estate well outside any town. Most of his constructs wander around the forest for a while before fading away without harming anyone."

"Then what about . . ." She brought her hand to her cheek, and thought it was unwise to ask about his scar. Men could be funny about those things.

"Nothing to do with anything except my own stupidity. I failed to control a newly-acquired bear."

Ouch. "Is that why you came with the bandits? To capture Loesie?"

"There were rumours of a magic-possessed woman coming this way, so he sent Sigvald. Possession is very rare and Sigvald is a brute, so I went with him, because I didn't think that a lone woman in the presence of bandits was going to end happily."

"What did you do to make those spiders vanish?"

"It's just a simple spell that people with air magic can do."

"Didn't look simple to me."

He stopped walking. "You know, you Saarlanders are all so ignorant about magic that even though some of you have a limited ability you wouldn't know what to do with it. One day, someone is going to come who knows how to use magic and wants to take control over your country's strategic location. You will be defenceless."

That may already have happened.

She met his eyes, but said nothing.

"Saarland needs court magicians."

She nodded, really confused now about what he was trying to tell her. Nothing he had said so far convinced her that he didn't know who Roald was. He came to conclusions similar to her own, and now—was he saying *Hey, if you need to employ a magician, I'm available?*

She wanted to believe he was being honest with her, about his father, about his mission to capture Loesie. He sounded too naïve, unbelievable for someone with as many powers as he seemed to have.

The little voice inside her said, *This is all a trap. You need to leave as soon as possible if you don't want to end up dead inside the ice cellar.*

They arrived in the upstairs corridor. Nellie opened the door to the kids' room while Johanna and Sylvan manoeuvred Loesie through. They dragged her onto the bed.

Sylvan left, and Nellie helped Johanna take Loesie's dress off.

Loesie's eyes were no longer white, and followed Johanna's hands as she undid the laces.

"Do you feel better?"

"What are we doing here?" Loesie asked.

"I just told you when we were coming up the stairs."

Loesie frowned.

"She's almost cured," Nellie said.

"I'm not sure. Loesie speaks in eastern dialect, and she doesn't seem to listen to anything we say."

"Well, she's better than before. I'm sure this man can cure her."

Johanna shrugged. She still didn't trust the duke. As some point she was going to have to ask him bluntly what his business was with an ice cellar full of dead bodies. Until she knew, and probably even after, she wouldn't trust either him or his son, who seemed all too keen to offer his services.

"You're sure you can handle being with her in the room?" Johanna asked.

"I can manage. A wife should be with her husband anyway."

Johanna vacillated between telling Nellie off for always worrying about what was appropriate and letting it go. In the end, the easy option won. She was too tired to argue.

Loesie was already half asleep, so Johanna went with Roald to the other bedroom.

Someone had been in to light the fire, which burned with a healthy glow. Neither Johanna nor Roald said anything when entering the room. Roald hadn't said much even at dinner or during that horrible magical performance. She worried about what went on in his head. Eventually, he would have questions about it.

When Johanna closed the door, sounds in the room became muffled. The room had a thick carpet and heavy curtains. It would have been quite cosy if not for the fact that the furniture was sparse and dusty.

Once, many people had lived in this house. What had happened?

A small table with a carafe of wine and two glasses on it stood near the hearth. The church frowned upon the consumption of alcohol, and wine had to be imported in Saarland, so there was rarely any at the table. She found it strange that other sections of the church allowed wine. It was as if all the districts had different interpretations of the book.

Johanna poured wine in the glasses. "I don't really know what to think of the duke. He seems kind enough, but . . ." She shrugged and went to the fire. Her hands were still cold from the magic, and she couldn't quite dispel the memory of those spiders. And then Sylvan's spell. Should she accept the help of the son of a man who had tried to kill his half-brother? He was right in that

Saarland needed a court magician. They needed many other people as well. It was high time that they found survivors and started establishing the position of the royal family.

Roald sat staring at some point across the room. Johanna picked up the cups.

"Roald, look at me."

He turned his head. "Oh yes, I love to look."

Not like that. Heavens, was that what he had been thinking all night? "No, that's not what I mean. I want to ask you a few things."

"Oh?"

He took the glass from her.

Johanna sat down and took a sip. The fluid's taste was quite sharp and it made a little burning track inside her all the way down to her stomach. "When you went away with the order in Burovia, were they people of the Church?"

"I don't like going to church. My father says I have to go. The monks want me to go every day, but I like much better to work in the fields. I get the horses, I feed the horses. I pick the grapes. I weed the garden."

"So this place was a monastery?"

He frowned at her.

"A monastery is where monks live and pray. You said they were monks."

"But it wasn't a monastery."

"There are no women in a monastery."

A slight frown. "Yes, it was like that and it's very sad, because there are no women to look at. You know these monks have never looked at a woman? They don't like talking about it either. Probably because they don't know."

For crying out loud. Was there anything he could get excited about other than women and the family tree of various royal families?

"The monks in this . . ." She almost said monastery again. ". . . place go to church?"

"Every day."

"What does the church look like?"

He frowned. "Like a church?"

"Is there anything in the church?"

"Benches to sit, and for the choir. They tried to get me to join the choir, but I don't like the music. It's boring and too slow, but I can't sing that slow. I get out of breath."

She chuckled. "Are there any statues in the church?"

"Like the one in the big church, with the dog-heads?"

"It has only one dog head, but yes, that's the one."

He frowned. "It has two."

"No, there is one. The other heads are the ghost and the holy god."

"There are two."

"One."

"Two."

Johanna realised: this might well be a different statue of the triune. She had not known Roald to be wrong about anything.

"So there is a statue like that in the big church in Saardam?" Would that church still be standing?

"Yes, I just said so."

"It's at the front of the church, with the pulpit to one side and—"

He shook his head. "It's in the middle and all the benches are around it."

Yes. A different church, obviously. Now she was getting somewhere. "Do you remember the names of any of the monks?"

"Peter."

"They were all named Peter?"

"No, there were others." He held up his hand and counted on his fingers. "David, Johan, Anselmus, Bernhard—"

"Was there one named Alexandre?"

He frowned. "He is not a monk. He is . . . ooohhh, you don't mess with him."

"If he's not a monk, then what is he?"

"He says he's a prince of Burovia, but I don't believe that, because the king has no sons."

No legitimate ones at any rate. Illegitimate ones were another matter.

With a lot of difficulty, she managed to get out of him that someone named Alexandre was also a guest at the order where he had stayed. It had been a church farm of sorts, where they also grew herbs for making concoctions. Other guests included two of Baron Uti's cousins, both of whom, Roald said, spent a lot of time in the dungeons as punishment for *being inebriated and disorderly*.

The place seemed like a home for troublesome royals. The young men were subjected to a punishing schedule of hard work and prayers when they weren't in the fields.

They had an elaborate system of punishments that seemed quite excessive. Lashes for a lot of minor transgressions like being late in church or forgetting to tidy one's bed, time in the dungeons for more serious missteps, such as failing to recite prayers properly or making fun of figures of authority. The most serious of crimes, blasphemy, attracted a punishment of a week in chains without food, and a hundred lashes every morning.

"They used a belt on me, not a chain, because of the scars." He said this proudly.

"You mean they locked you in the cellar and hit you every day?"

He lifted his shirt. "See? No scars."

Johanna looked at that bronzed skin with renewed awe. "Why did they punish you?"

"They said Prince Richert of Estland stole bread from the kitchens but he didn't. I know that for a fact. Because I stole the bread for Tomas, who was sick and couldn't come to the hall to eat. The monk wouldn't believe me so I called him a prick."

Somewhere in that distant mind of his was a very strong sense of justice.

"What was this Alexandre doing there?"

"He was friends with the monks. He never made his own bed. He never worked. I wasn't afraid of him, but many people were."

Alexandre, Roald further informed her, came from the Burovian river town of Lisseau. This was on the Saar River and Johanna had been there. A pretty town, not very big, but it did have a fair bit of money. Apparently the Nielands used creditors in Lisseau to finance their bid to go into ocean trade.

This whole situation was becoming more complex by the day.

Eventually, the fire died and the glasses were empty. The wine had made a warm spot in her stomach. Somehow, the problems of the world seemed far away and not so important. It was comfortable and warm in this room, and Loesie would get better. They would get out of here, and would never know about the bodies in the ice cellar. Maybe the reason they were there wasn't for her to know anyway. She put her glass down. "We should go to sleep."

Roald turned to her, an eager expression on his face. "Now do I get to look at you?"

"If you want." She didn't feel like any awkward acrobatics, but he was her husband now, so it was his right to ask.

She let herself out of the horribly stiff dress. Roald's

intense gaze made her feel uncomfortable so she went to the window, dressed in her underclothes, and pushed the curtain aside a crack. It was very dark outside, the sky spotted with stars. The room was at the front of the house, looking out over the clipped bushes and neat beds of the gardens.

"I like looking at you." Roald had come up from behind and put his hands on her hips. His palms felt warm through the underdress. He tugged at the fabric. "Take this one off, too."

Johanna slipped the underdress over her head. A cold draft from the window made her shiver. She pulled the string around her waist and dropped her drawers. Roald stepped a little back, staring at her.

"Yes, I really like looking at you."

Johanna took off his jacket and undid the buttons to his shirt. He sat down on the bed, pulling her onto his lap and pressing his face between her breasts.

"They're so soft." His breath tickled over her naked skin.

He slid his hand over her back, pressing her closer to him. She could feel him through his trousers. The thought of that first night came with a slight shudder.

"Wait." She rose, undid his belt and peeled open the front of his trousers. His member stood straight up, like an overgrown gherkin. And thinking about gherkins made her laugh.

"Heeeee!"

He pulled her back on his lap, nuzzling the white skin on her belly. She breathed the scent of his hair. It was getting quite long and unruly.

"You're quite tanned. Did you spend a lot of time outdoors?"

"All the time. They had cows. Real ones, not sea cows. I learnt to milk them. I worked in the field, harvesting grapes. The monks make wine."

"You liked that kind of work?"

"It was nice. My father says I have to be nice to all these boring people. Do I really have to? They don't like me."

Johanna chuckled, and then a feeling of sadness came over her. "Yes, you have to be nice to them." At least the ones who were still alive.

He leaned back on his elbows. "I want you to touch me now."

"Shift a bit further back."

He did. The whole thing was strange, an oddly rational and mechanical process. People said she was meant to feel something while doing this. *Like you really want it,* Augustina had confided, but she felt nothing.

Johanna climbed onto the bed, put one leg over him, took his member, lifted it up in the right position and pushed down. He went deep into her. He groaned.

"You find that pleasant."

"Ooooh, very nice." He rocked his hips.

"Don't do that, because it hurts me."

He frowned. "It hurts?"

"Not like this, but it does when you try to lift me in the air."

"Oh." He frowned. "Does that mean we can't do it anymore?"

"No, it doesn't mean that at all. Just that I would rather you didn't try to lift me off the bed anymore."

"Oh." His frown deepened.

A waft of cold air drifted through the room, making Johanna's naked skin crawl with goosebumps.

"But hurting people is bad."

"It doesn't hurt if you stay like this." She leaned on her outstretched arms on either side of his shoulders and rocked backwards and forwards. For a while neither of them said anything. Roald leaned his head back in the pillow, his eyes closed and mouth slightly open.

Each time she rocked, he gave a soft groan.

She wanted to feel what he felt, because she didn't under-stand this. Helena said that it was easier if you pretended to enjoy it, and that pretending to enjoy it sometimes led to enjoying it. And Johanna figured that she'd better learn to enjoy it or otherwise this part of her life would be very miserable.

She didn't want to be miserable, she wanted to enjoy it. She wanted to feel something.

Johanna kept rocking her hips. She closed her eyes. Why hadn't she noticed how tight it was, and how each time she pushed forward, she rubbed a very sensitive spot?

Roald grabbed her thighs with white-knuckled hands. He groaned with each time she rocked back. Johanna remem-bered the noise he had made the previous time. She had the vague notion to tell him to be quiet, but part of her didn't care, and that part was taking over her mind. She rocked harder and faster, because it was pleasant, and because she was married and they could do this.

And then Roald arched his back and did his *huhhhh!* thing, almost lifting her. It would have hurt but she didn't feel it anymore, he was that deep inside her.

He relaxed, his chest heaving with fast breaths.

"That was good," he said.

She nodded. She didn't think it was as good as it could be, but this was obviously something they could work on. Some-thing that didn't require him to use words.

She went to sleep next to him, in the warm hollow made by his body in the mattress and enveloped by the peculiar smell of his seed that flowed out of her and made wet patches on the sheets and her underdress. She didn't care. He might have snored, but she didn't notice. She had done her duty. The future of the Carmine House would grow inside her.

~

Johanna woke up sometime in the night when it was still pitch dark. She lifted her head off the pillow, aware of the coldness on her back. Roald sat up in bed.

From somewhere outside came an unfamiliar *crunch, crunch* sound.

"What's that noise?" Her tongue wouldn't cooperate.

Roald didn't reply, but she recognised the sound. Footsteps on gravel. Horses.

At this time of the night?

She climbed out of bed and tiptoed over to the window. A cold draft worked its fingers around her legs and under her underdress.

A half-moon had come up. It faint blue light silvered the perfectly-tended garden, the hedges, the clipped trees, the benches and ponds. A group of people stood on the drive, one of them leading a horse by the reins. The animal tossed its head and snorted as if it had been running.

The other two people looked like they were house servants, but not Hans or the woman Johanna had seen. The three spoke with raised voices, too far away for Johanna to hear.

Roald came to stand behind her, a warm presence at her back.

"Who is that?" he asked.

"I don't know."

"Does he always receive guests in the middle of the night?"

"I have no idea, but it's odd." Especially since there would have been little light for the traveller's horse to see by.

One of the servants took the horse in the direction of the stables; the other accompanied the traveller up the steps to the house.

At the top of the stairs another man came out of the house. Johanna recognised the long hair of Sylvan. He met the newcomer on the paving in front of the door. The two spoke briefly. Sylvan gestured wildly with his hands and then the other man raised his voice. Sylvan shouted something at him. The visitor walked past him towards the main door. As he did so, he raised his head, and Johanna could see his face.

It was Kylian.

CHAPTER 12

J OHANNA AND ROALD went back to bed. Roald fell asleep immediately, but Johanna was too disturbed to sleep. What in all the heavens was Kylian doing here?

She still saw him on that night Saardam burned, first when their eyes met across the crowded hall, when she could feel his magic, then him wanting to dance with her, having followed her, perhaps, into the deserted gallery. Admitting that he could sense her magic. The kiss—no, she didn't want to think about that. Then he'd asked her to come with him to Florisheim. And then, when the fire started, he'd jumped over the wall and disappeared without trace *while his father was still in the hall.*

She could still feel the moment his lips touched hers. Her overwhelming reaction had been one of disgust, and then fascination. Wanting to know more, but knowing that the knowledge was forbidden until she was married. She had never questioned what he was doing there or why he had fled so quickly.

Or why the memories made her feel hot.

Now that she was married, any thought of him was

fraught with danger. If she came face-to-face with him here, he might bring up their nightly encounter at the palace. So mysterious, dangerous, inappropriate . . . Whatever she did, those thoughts would just not die.

You're better off never seeing him again, said the little voice inside her that sounded like Nellie.

She clamped the pillow over her head. She didn't want to think about him. She never wanted to see him again. Why couldn't she just go back to sleep like Roald?

Johanna forced herself to calm down, but those thoughts would not go away. Roald snored and kept jiggling his leg. The mattress was so soft that she kept sliding into him. Johanna tossed and turned and grumbled under her breath that she was going to sleep on the floor, all of which had precisely no effect. She might as well have been talking to a sack of grain for the notice he took of her.

Eventually she fell back asleep when a faint glow of dawn coloured the little strip of sky she could see between the curtains, and a few birds made tentative warm-up noises for the morning chorus. She woke up with a shock when the sunlight flooded into the room. She rolled onto her back and lay staring at the plaster flowers on the ceiling.

Oh, by the heavens, her head felt like it was stuffed with wool.

This sleeping in the same bed thing would have to improve a lot or she was going to get her own bedroom. A blackbird sang on the roof with another one answering further away. There were no city noises, and no noises from within the house.

Someone walked *crunch, crunch, crunch* on the gravel of the drive.

Roald gave a startled snore.

Johanna threw back the cover with more vigour than necessary and pushed the heavy curtain aside, but it was only the stablehand Karl carrying a bucket of scraps down the lane, out to the chicken coop. The sky was soft blue and sunlight beat down on this side of the house, edging Karl's hair in a golden glow. He had sail ears.

Johanna let the curtain fall and went in search of her clothes. Would the duke expect her to wear his dress again today? She picked up the heavy fabric, cringing at the stiffness of the bodice. The farm dress which she had worn since the day after the burning of Saardam needed mending and washing, and she couldn't imagine wearing that to breakfast with a duke, especially if Kylian might be there.

Kylian.

Now, in the brightness of morning, it seemed like a dream that she had even seen him. She must have been mistaken. After all, if the duke had tried to kill Kylian's father, and even Roald had learned of that plot while he was in Burovia, why would he visit the duke's castle alone in the middle of the night?

Because Kylian wants his father killed as well?

So—to sum up: the burning of Saardam was an attack on Baron Uti after several failed assassination attempts by his half-brother. The burning was magical, and she had seen and felt Kylian's magic. He could have—no, he couldn't. The fire demons had been leaping over the roofs before Kylian ran. He could never have been in control of those beasts all the way from the palace.

That was a comforting thought. See? Kylian had nothing to do with it. Maybe even the baron had nothing to do with it. They were just guests of the royal family.

Oh, her head hurt from thinking about all this. Why didn't Roald worry about all this? Why did he lay there snoring when she couldn't sleep? Worse, why did she let this stuff keep her awake?

She should go and check on Loesie.

Never mind the duke's fancy clothes, she flung on her old farm dress and went to the door.

"You need to help me." Roald had gotten out of bed and stood with his arms wide, like a doll wanting to be dressed up.

Johanna whirled around. "Can't you dress yourself at all?" Seriously, he expected her to be available for him, kept her awake all night with his snoring and expected her to dress him as if he were a toddler?

He managed to look confused.

"It's not that hard to learn. I have to go and check Loesie." She went out the door and she had to do her best not to slam it.

As she entered the corridor, Nellie just came up the stairs, looking awfully awake. "Oh, I was just going to check if you were up yet."

"How is Loesie?"

"Still asleep. I left her like that. No need to wake her up."

"You're very cheerful, Nellie." Way too cheerful after such a night.

"Isn't the weather nice today?"

"Uhm . . . yeah?" *Have you forgotten that we have an exorcism to do today, somewhere in that horrible forest?* "How long have you been downstairs?"

"I got up just after sunrise, as I normally do. I went in search of a chapel or shrine for prayers of thanks that we've survived so far. I couldn't see any in the house so I went into the garden. I met a very helpful young man there—"

Kylian. "Did he have hair the colour of autumn leaves? And chestnut brown eyes?"

"Why, yes, he did. Do you know him?"

"He's Kylian prince of Gelre, Baron Uti's son."

Nellie's eyes widened. "You're kidding."

"Do I ever kid?"

"All the time, Mistress Johanna."

"When it's serious?" Then she thought about something else. "What did you tell him about us?"

"What do you mean?"

"Did you tell him where you are from and how we got here?"

"Well, he wanted to know, so I said we came through the forest."

"Did you give him our names?"

Nellie's cheeks had gone bright red. "No, I didn't. You said that we shouldn't, days ago, so I didn't."

"Did he ask?"

"He asked if I was alone and I said that a few friends had come with me. Is there a problem, Mistress Johanna? Why do you mistrust people so?"

Johanna really, really didn't like Nellie's red cheeks. That was a sure sign that something was going on.

"Is he downstairs at breakfast?"

"Oh no, he said he had to go."

Go where? "He didn't even speak to the duke?"

"I don't know. Why are you asking me all these things? I don't know anything. I met him, I talked to him briefly. He was kind and I had no reason to question him."

"Did the duke say anything about his visit?"

"No, he didn't." She gave Johanna another *what do you need to know this for* stare. "Anyway, breakfast is ready."

"I'll check on Roald." Because *he* hadn't come out of the room either. And someone needed to wake up Loesie or bring her some breakfast.

Johanna went into the bedroom where it smelled of male sweat. Roald sat helpless on the bed, looking at his shirt which he held in white-knuckled hands on top of his knees.

"Come on, let's go to breakfast. The duke is expecting us downstairs. Are you hungry? There will probably be honey."

He said nothing and that was strange, because the mention of honey should have him jumping at the door.

"Roald?"

A sob.

Johanna closed the door and crossed the room to him. He sat with his shoulders hunched. When she knelt in front of him, he pressed his balled fists to his face, still clutching the shirt.

"What is the matter?"

He wailed. "You're angry with me."

"I'm not angry with you."

"Yes, you are!"

"Shhh, quiet. Behave like a prince. You don't want people to hear that you're crying." Or worse, Kylian to realise who was upstairs and tell the duke.

"I don't care. You're angry with me. I'm a bad husband."

"No, you're not."

"Yes I am!" He was swaying from one side to the other as if in a trance.

"Roald, please." She eased the shirt from his hands, forcing him to look at her by manoeuvring herself into his line of vision. She grabbed his shoulders so that he would stop that horrible swaying.

His eyes focused and widened.

"Don't do that, please."

He said nothing. His entire body shook with sobs.

"Keep calm. No one is angry with you." *Please, keep yourself together. I need you to be calm.*

She closed her arms around his shoulders. The naked skin felt cool to the touch. "Come, hold your hands out. I'll help you put on your clothes."

Roald calmed a bit, but his hands still trembled. One day, she would teach him how to dress himself, but for now, it wasn't worth worrying about. Johanna wrestled him into his shirt and jacket. The farm clothes he had worn coming here were too dirty to wear to a duke's breakfast. She would ask if their clothes could be washed.

Not much later they both met Nellie in the corridor. While Nellie wore the duke's dress, Johanna had opted to stay in her old farm clothes.

Nellie's face was disapproving. "Mistress Johanna, are you going to breakfast like that?"

"I don't trust this man and until I know where all these expensive clothes come from, I'm not going to wear them anymore."

"They used to belong to his wife. He told me."

And where was his wife now? The ice cellar?

She didn't want to think about it. She needed the duke to return Loesie to her normal form, but after that, they'd be out of here as soon as possible.

In the dining room, they found the duke alone at the dinner table. The dour-faced woman had just brought in a tray with boiled eggs, jam, bread, yellow butter and honey, which she was setting out on the table.

Everyone sat down in the same positions as last night.

The duke smiled at her. "I hope you slept well." Like this, he looked so much like a friendly old man that it was easy to see how Nellie was fooled into trusting him.

"There was a lot of noise outside the window last night," Johanna said. "I heard a horse coming up the drive."

"Karl the stablehand goes out to swim the horses most mornings."

And he was going to lie about it, too.

"Nellie said you had a visitor?"

"Did she?"

Nellie's cheeks went red. "I met this nice young man this morning when I went in search of a chapel or shrine."

"Oh, that was just my nephew."

"He arrived in the middle of the night?"

"He comes here at all hours so often I almost consider him part of the furniture." The duke chuckled. Johanna studied his face, but saw no sign that he considered this an uncomfortable subject for discussion.

"Did he bring any news? Did he come from Florisheim?"

"He did. He says that many refugees are still arriving in town and things are a bit crowded over there. I'm sending some people with him to help keep the order."

"People from Saarland?"

"Yes, many, and also Estland."

"We'd like to join them as soon as possible."

"It would be unwise to travel into the forest with your friend in this state."

"We were going to do something about that today, right?"

"Yes, certainly." He looked uneasy. "Understand, though, that exorcism is not a precise science. Even if she is completely cleared, there is some danger of lingering traces of magic. There are bands of rogue magicians in the forest. There are people who would kill you and eat you. I'm not even talking about the ghouls and other magical creatures."

"You could send some bandits with us."

"It's not that simple."

"They work for you, don't they?"

"They don't. I pay them sometimes to keep an eye on who enters this area and what they are doing here. As you can see, we are only a few in this house and I am quite poor in health. I cannot ride anymore, and have to rely on others to check my lands. Our holding is very large and much of it is useless forest."

Johanna cast a sharp glance at Roald, in case he was going to divulge his vast knowledge about the Baron's family's sordid family details. She couldn't help but think how he'd lain in bed under her, his eyes closed. It was scary and wonderful that she could do this to someone who was socially awkward and incapable of dressing himself.

Roald remained silent.

"What about your son?" After last night, Johanna hadn't seen him anymore.

"He cannot do these things alone. He has a need to go into the forest. His magic of living things needs him to roam in nature. I suspect he's gone riding this morning."

Or maybe he just had a profound dislike for Kylian.

"What are you going to do today?"

"Yesterday, I was able to break some of the demon's wards that affected your friend. What we'll do today is try to coax the demon out of her."

"How does that work?"

"There is passive coaxing, which we tried yesterday with the wine. Demons love wine. Unfortunately, they're usually determined to stay where they are. Sometimes they've been inside that person for such a long time that they're afraid to come out. At other times they're under specific orders to stay. Just offering something they like doesn't always have the desired effect."

"Vomiting spiders? Is that a desired effect?" Johanna shuddered.

"It is part of breaking a ward that magicians often use to secure their demons. Really, child, you know so little about magic. It is a wonder you have survived the trip here."

I'm not a child. "Then tell us."

"Well, it is like this: magic belongs to nature. It resides in wood, in water, in wind, in the soil—"

"In fire?"

He gave her a sharp look. "Yes, fire, too. The original people with those kinds of magic lived on land where the elements displayed these types of magic. The magic itself is contained in lines that run through the land. They may be in the soil or in the water or in the air. The creek you would have followed for much of your journey has a strong water magic line. The people who lived on its banks and drank its water became imbued with magic, which they passed on to other generations. But as people move around more, magic has become muddled. People from different estates have moved elsewhere and intermarried."

The sour-faced maid came in, asking if they had finished eating.

"Yes, take all the plates away."

"We need some breakfast for our friend who is still upstairs."

"Certainly." The maid set aside a plate with two thick slices of bread and a little jar of jam.

The duke waited until she was gone. "On this estate, we have water lines crossing with earth lines and tree lines. My grandfather built the living tunnels that lead up to the junction. Everything converges in this one point. He was such a strong tree magician that to this day, the trees obey his spells."

A chill went down Johanna's back. Was tree magic the same as willow magic?

"And this junction is where we have to take Loesie?"

"It is, because that is where I can best tap the magic that I need to fully drive the demon from her soul. Let us go." He picked up his walking stick and used it to push himself from the table. Nellie tried to assist him but he would have no help. "What do you think I am? An old man?" He smiled and winked at her.

He shuffled into the hallway, where he started explaining to Roald about all the portraits that hung there and who was related to whom and who had built which part of the house.

Johanna and Nellie climbed the stairs to get Loesie. Nellie was carrying the plate with the bread and the jam.

Behind them, the duke's voice echoed in the cavernous hall. ". . . and then that one over there, that's my great-grand-uncle Willem, who bought the neighbouring landholding . . ."

"Do you think we're doing the right thing?" Johanna asked in a low voice as soon as they were in the upstairs corridor.

"I thought you knew about all this magic?"

"I know enough to know that I know nothing. Should we trust him?"

"It seems to me that if there is anyone who can help the poor girl, it's this man."

"I'm not so certain that he does it to help us. He wants the demon, and I'm worried about what he wants to do with it."

"He told us: study demons. He's certainly a bit odd, but I can't see him doing any harm. He's an old man, and not good of health. You're very distrusting, Mistress Johanna."

"Well, yes. I want to like him. He *seems* a nice old man, But Roald told me that the duke has tried to murder his half-brother Baron Uti a few times and . . ." She hesitated, but could not bring herself to mention the bodies. Loesie needed to be helped. In her current state, Loesie was a danger to everyone, including herself. Loesie knew who had done this to her. Likely, Loesie knew who led the people who had burned Saardam, and telling Nellie what she knew might not only make Nellie afraid, but the knowledge might end up in places where it would be harmful. Kylian seemed to have a knack for extracting information out of girls.

They found Loesie on the bed, staring at the ceiling.

She looked up when Johanna and Nellie came in.

"We're going to help you today," Nellie said in a voice that sounded too cheerful.

Loesie gave Johanna a hard and cool stare. "What are we doing here?" That same question again. How many times had she asked it already?

"We're going into the forest," Johanna said. "Let's get you dressed."

Loesie just repeated, "What are we doing here?"

Johanna shivered. Somehow, she preferred Loesie unable to talk but with some of her wits.

Loesie's old black dress was definitely beyond wearing outside, so they dressed her in one of the duke's dresses. Nellie had put the bread on a little table next to the hearth, which Loesie ate while Nellie tried to bring some order to her hair.

Loesie sat like a doll while Nellie yanked at the knots. "You're going to have to cut some of these out. This is just terrible."

Where previously Loesie would have gotten angry, because she didn't like anyone commenting on what she looked like, she only repeated, "What are we doing here?"

Nellie managed to get Loesie's hair into some sort of bun, and then they helped Loesie down the stairs. It was as if every time Johanna touched Loesie, she seemed more fragile.

This thing is killing her, like having wasting sickness.

In the hall, the duke was still talking to Roald about his family. Roald let his gaze wander over the walls and ceiling, but Johanna had no doubt that he heard—and would remember—everything the duke said.

"Ah, there you are. Karl has brought the wagon. Come with me."

He started for the door, but Johanna held Nellie back.

"You don't have to watch this, Nellie. You're probably better off waiting here. It could get really nasty."

Nellie didn't protest.

"I will go with you," Roald said.

"Stay here with Nellie," Johanna said. Whatever was going to happen in that forest was not going be pleasant.

Roald didn't protest either. The two of them looked forlorn in that huge and empty hall.

An open wagon with a single horse stood in front of the steps. The stablehand Karl came up the steps and helped Loesie into the back seat. He offered her a cloak, but she didn't want it.

Johanna gladly took the offered cloak. The sun might be out, but the air was crisp. Next, Karl helped the duke into the wagon. He settled on the bench next to her, with a blanket over his legs and clutching the walking stick between his knees.

Johanna turned around to check on Loesie. In the space between the seats stood a crate covered with a dark red cloth and the cage made of rusty iron.

Karl jumped into the driver's seat. With a flick of the reins, they were off, along the gravel drive and the tree-lined path. This was why the network of lanes was so extensive: so that the duke could go for rides.

They rode out into the forest to the far side of the castle. A fine haze still hung between the trees and over the water of the lake. A swan glided gracefully over the water, barely stirring the surface with a ripple.

Oak trees grew on the sides of the lake, big ones with twisted and knotted trunks. The field between the trees was a riot of buttercups, daisies, dandelions, wild carrot and soft purple flowers on slender stems.

The horse trotted at a brisk pace, so she guessed that their destination couldn't be too far away, but it was hard to judge distance in this undulating country.

They went over a hill and into the forest. Pale sunlight made the fresh leaves on the trees look bright green, although a haze still lingered between the trees. Johanna looked for signs, but saw no traces of magic.

Loesie sat in the back of the wagon, observing the countryside. Her face was pale and drawn, the skin on her bone-thin arms grey and ghost-like. She had given up asking what they were doing here and Johanna was glad about that. She couldn't imagine how frightening it must be to have something else possess your soul and drown out your own thoughts. Then a disturbing thought: Loesie was meant to survive this exorcism, wasn't she?

The horses followed a path that ran along a creek that fed the lake. The watercourse meandered between trees, through thickets and marshy bogs. The water was so clear that you could see the white sand at the bottom.

They came to a field with a farmhouse. The orchard bloomed on the far side of the house. Cows grazed in the meadow. It was all so peaceful that it was hard to believe that there were major veins of magic nearby.

Then up another hill between huge gnarled oak trees with thick and knobbly trunks. Several trees were hollow and had lost large branches over the years, leaving gaping maws of darkness where Johanna could almost see pairs of eyes staring back at her.

"These trees are older than the estate itself," the duke said. "They are hundreds of years old."

Johanna believed it, too. In the back of her mind rose the soft whisper of voices. The very forest was alive with magic. A breeze brought a chill wind that made Johanna shiver.

"The tree line passes here," the duke said. "This is why those trees get so old. The line goes from here, through the field over there to the other side of the hill." He pointed with his walking stick.

"Do all trees have memories? In Saarland, it's just the willow trees and willow wood."

"That's because they grow close to the water, and that water comes from here. Magic spreads all over the world."

"Does all magic come from around here? Everything seems to have magic."

"No, magic is a far eastern thing. You may think that this countryside is alive with magic, but we have few strong magicians. In the far east, everyone is a strong magician."

Johanna thought of the tales told by seafaring traders of the evils that lay around the horn. "But the stories of sea creatures are fables, certainly?"

"I don't know about sea creatures, that's the domain of the sailors, but I do know of some people who attempted to go to the east overland. I don't know the names of the creatures the easterners have, but they are made of pure magic. If they want ill—and why not, because who can stop them?—they can overrun the entire world and reduce us to slaves. We do not want that to happen, right?"

Johanna thought back to the ball on the night of the fire. Father's colleague Master Deim had been saying similar things.

Everyone was saying it: *If the people from the far east came . . .*

Well, if they did, they would find this region's main port in a big mess, ruled by a puppet from a church that taught that magic didn't exist.

The wagon crested the hill and entered an area where five tree-lined lanes joined. Between the straight and slender beech trunks, Johanna had a view over a green meadow which sloped down on the other side. Karl pulled the reins and the horse slowed.

Johanna looked around. "Is this the place?"

A cold breeze blew in from the opposite direction, and it contained a prick of magic. Wailing voices that cried of misery and death.

She shivered despite the nice weather.

The five-point intersection looked an extremely unlikely location for a magical junction.

"No, not here, but most of us will have to continue on foot. We need to go down there." The duke pointed at the meadow.

A network of dark hedges ran through undulating grassy land, all joining at a hillock in the centre. No, they were not hedges. She followed the closest of them uphill, where it branched off a lane that joined the intersection. They were *paths* hidden under living tunnels of branches. Trees forced by magic to grow in tunnel shape to hide the path underneath. All these tunnels met up in a larger, dome-shaped junction, also formed out of tortured trees.

Johanna shivered. Who treated trees like this? She wanted to run to the trees and free them if she knew how.

At the mouth of the tunnel waited a man on a horse, his face shaded inside the hood of his cloak.

"You came," the duke said.

The man lowered the hood. It was Sylvan, his scarred face humourless. "Did you ever think I wouldn't?"

"I can never be sure with you."

Karl brought the wagon to a complete halt. He got down from the driver's seat and helped the duke down, and then Johanna. Sylvan also dismounted.

Karl took care of Sylvan's horse.

Loesie in the wagon couldn't walk and now Johanna understood why he had chosen such a simple wagon. A bigger one would not have fitted through this tunnel.

Sylvan took the horse by the reins and led the way into the tunnel.

CHAPTER 13

A S SOON AS Johanna set foot on the path, voices whispered with the wind, the words lilting and mysterious. The leaves rustled as if reaching for her. They were bursting with stories. They were in pain. They struggled against their magic-enforced shape. They wailed *Set us free, set us free*.

The chill that took hold of her went to her bones.

The duke, walking behind the wagon, concentrated on where he put his feet and his walking stick on the uneven ground. Both he and Loesie in the cart showed no signs of being affected; neither did Sylvan.

Johanna had to restrain herself from running away. She had to get out of here. Something bad was going to happen.

But the duke kept walking slowly, with his cane going *tap, tap, tap* on the uneven ground. Once the path had been paved, but the baked clay bricks had crumbled so that the surface was uneven and pitted with holes. He tapped the ground with his walking stick, as if seeking out safe places to put his feet.

His breath came quite heavy and at times he had to stop for a while.

"I ask my son to come here, usually," he said during one such stop. "He can do most things that need to be done regularly."

"What sort of things?"

"Setting wards and renewing protections. Seriously, girl, what do they teach you in that so-called enlightened town of yours? Does no one protect the town or even their property with wards? You have the gift. Are you going to tell me that all of your life, you have never done anything with it?"

"The church forbids magic."

"The church forbids *dark* magic. There is a big difference."

"In Saarland any magic is dark. Also, isn't that what we're coming out here for? Exorcism? Isn't that dark magic?"

"Yes. Dark magic has touched your friend. There is no way to undo dark magic other than with dark magic. In fact, the term dark magic is a poorly-chosen one. It simply means magic that requires active involvement. Not all of it is dark, or bad. The darkness is not in the magic, it is in the user."

A gust of wind made the branches whistle in high-pitched voices. It was as if someone screamed a warning. *Get away from him! He'll turn you into a toad!*

"Nooo!" Johanna clamped her hands over her ears.

Set us free, set us free, set us free.

Sylvan said something to his father which Johanna didn't hear. Neither of them laughed, as the bandits would have done.

She didn't know what to think anymore. One the one hand, she wanted to trust this man. On the other hand . . . she and Loesie were at his mercy. If he wanted ill, there would be no stopping him.

They had come to the top of the hillock in the middle of the web of tree tunnels. Seven tunnels met each other here in a space that could best be described as a cathedral of trees.

In the middle was a circle of stone paving with, in the middle, a stone altar. It was an old-looking thing, made from ancient stone. The top bore carvings, but age had worn away at the stone, so it was hard to see what the image depicted.

"This is where the magic lines meet." The duke smiled. "The water line runs from here to there." He pointed. "The earth line runs across the meadow. The wood line runs down the path we've just come on. I trust you've heard voices or felt magic?"

Johanna nodded. The whispering voices in the back of her head would not go away.

"My grandfather had this planted. My wife and I were married here."

The voices screamed in her ears, the words no longer audible. The chill of the wind took her breath away.

But the sun was still shining and the leaves on the trees didn't move visibly. The horse showed no signs of being disturbed by magic, and horses were normally very skittish. Loesie was also not more disturbed than usual. Was it just her?

Sylvan stopped the cart. The duke took the reins while Sylvan helped Loesie down from the wagon. He picked her up in his arms and set her on top of the stone table, then he lifted the cage and crate out of the wagon and put them on the ground.

He took the reins from his father and led the horse away. The wind carried the sound of the horse's footsteps on the eroded brick paving.

"Well, we may start," the duke said, breaking the tense silence.

He uncovered the crate and unloaded a number of items. A tall, long-necked bottle, half-filled with a dark, sloshing fluid. A gold-encrusted goblet. A sheep's skull. Johanna remembered the face of the Reverend Romulus. *You want an exorcist,* he had said. Well, she had found one, and now that he was about to start, she wondered if this was such a good idea. Actually, she was sure it *wasn't* such a good idea, because even Sylvan admitted that his father didn't always get it right.

But it was too late for all of that now.

The duke unstoppered the bottle and poured some of the fluid into the goblet. Then he slowly walked around the stone table, pouring drops of it on the ground until he had emptied the goblet. The wind brought a scent of sourness that made the hair on Johanna's arms stand up. *Like vomit.*

The duke met her eyes. "Dark magic is nothing more than us using the magic we have been born with to create more of the same. Your magic is wood, so you should be able to make things grow in whatever fashion you want."

"It that what your grandfather did? Force the trees to grow this way?"

It was a most hideous thing to do. Tree torture.

"It is up to us to control nature, or else nature will control us."

He hobbled back to the cart, leaned his walking stick to it, and produced a box. Inside lay a couple of burning coals. He held a dry stick against the heat and blew. The wood started smoking. He lifted the stick in front of his face. A curl of smoke rose from its tip.

"I need to warn you. My magic is fire, so you may see some strange phenomena soon."

Fire magic. There had been fire demons on the roofs of Saardam on the day the city burned. Kylian had jumped over the fence as soon as he saw those. Had the duke been in the city? He said he rarely travelled except along the tree-lined lanes of his estate. Maybe they weren't as far from the river as she thought. Maybe he'd come with his half-brother—the one he'd supposedly tried to kill? The situation was getting more confusing all the time.

The duke turned the burning stick upside down. An orange flame erupted from its burning end, and crept over the length of the wood.

The duke blew and fanned the flames. Fire licked his fingers, but it didn't seem to bother him. Sylvan gave him a torch made from a stick with oil-drenched straw. The flames went *wooof* when he held the burning stick underneath. He swung the torch from side to side to fan the flames, scattering bits of burning straw on his clothes and in his hair. Smoke rose from a patch on the shoulder of his jacket, that was spreading now, with a ring of tiny flames.

Just as Johanna wanted to say something about it, he flung the torch into the air towards the "roof" of the tree cathedral.

Something made a terrible screeching noise, like an animal about to be killed. Johanna clamped her hands over her ears. "Stop it!"

The duke held his outstretched hands towards the torch, which hung in mid-air, spewing flames in all directions. He spoke harsh-sounding words in a low voice.

As the torch fell, the flames detached themselves from the wood end and shaped themselves into some kind of *creature* that moved of its own accord. It grew a long bushy tail, an elongate body and four short legs, and a rounded snout with two pointy ears with tufts of fire-hair at the top.

A squirrel. It hopped through the air, and paused on the duke's outstretched hand to look around. The tail twitched, leaking bits of fire. Then it ran down his arm, setting fire to his jacket in its wake. It ran across the ground, leaving a trail of singed grass, to the trunk of one of the imprisoned trees.

There was that horrible screech again and now she understood what it was: the wood's fear of this creature. Johanna shivered. A gust of wind tore between the trees, making the branches whistle.

The squirrel stopped, sat on its hind legs and sniffed the air.

The duke called a few words in that harsh, magical language and the creature ran back to the stone table. It sniffed the ground where he had poured the wine, following the trail of drops around the table. And around and around.

Loesie sat up, her eyes wide, more alert than Johanna had seen her. Her gaze followed the fire squirrel around the table, quite alarmed, Johanna thought.

Why were Loesie's clothes and the stone around her wet?

Wait—water dripped from above. *From the trees.* Loesie's magic was wood, and the trees were keeping her safe from the fire.

The single squirrel had split into two squirrels, running around and around with fire trailing from their bushy tails. The trees leaked water. Whenever it fell on a squirrel, there was a hiss and a cloud of steam.

The squirrels ran faster and faster until they merged into a blur of fire. With each round, their numbers doubled. There were eight and then sixteen, and then she lost count. Their fiery bodies blurred into one another. The air chilled. It was as if the sun dimmed and the wind picked up, whipping up the flames erupting from the many squirrel tails. Loesie sat motionless in this spectacle.

Johanna became aware of a strange noise, like a colony of bees trapped in a box. The extinguished torch had fallen on the ground next to the stone table. It trembled and jiggled. Little buds sprung from the handle of the torch. They grew into tendrils. Leaves sprouted. The twigs curled and twined around the base of the table. The vines pushed themselves up the side of the table and grew to the top of the heavy slab that covered it. They grew around Loesie's legs, around the bottle that still stood there, up her arms and through her hair.

The fire squirrels ran up the vines, seeding flames in their wake. The vines grew and grew as if trying to outpace the squirrels. Each time a vine burnt, a new one sprang up. They covered Loesie in layer upon layer of tightly-twisted vines. They grew up her legs, covered her body, her arms, grew through her hair, until her entire body was covered in vines. The squirrels ran up and down the vines, leaving fire in their wake. The vines regrew each time the fire had passed.

The duke stood with his hands outstretched and his eyes closed. His face was red, glistening with sweat. He urged the squirrels on, faster and faster. They still multiplied, but not as fast as before.

The vines combined into thicker branches that no longer had leaves. A solid cage of wood protected Loesie and the demon that possessed her.

"Sylvan!" the duke yelled.

A gust of wind fanned the flames, eating through the foliage. Sylvan stood with his hands outstretched. The wind obeyed him as it had when they were crossing the sand dunes.

The flames spread until they covered the entire tangle of vines. The fire belched thick clouds of smoke. The duke stepped into them, yelling incantations at the top of his voice. The roaring of the fire almost drowned him out.

He sang and chanted, waving his arms. The fire grew. Something soft hit Johanna's shoulder, and then her head, and her arm. Dead and shrivelled leaves rained down from the tree roof. The heat seared her skin.

"Loesie!" she called.

Her friend was in the middle of that inferno, protected by a layer of vines that were slowly and certainly eaten by flames. Great gouts of sparks gushed from the fire.

"The cage! Get the cage!" the duke shouted.

As soon as Sylvan stopped fanning the wind and picked up the iron cage, the fire dimmed.

His father took the cage from him, heavily leaning on his walking stick. "Go, keep the fire going." He inched forward until the flames swallowed him.

Johanna turned to Sylvan, but he took no notice of her. He waved his hands. He chanted at the top of his voice. The fire roared. Gouts of flame erupted from the burning vines. Even the stone slab burned.

Then there was a rush of air towards the fire, followed by a sharper rush away from the fire. With an almighty roar, the knot of vines exploded. A huge fireball tore around the tree cathedral, dragging a white-hot object behind it. The fireball burst free through the cathedral roof and into the air. The glowing object bounced along the ground a few times and came to a halt. It was the metal cage, its door open, empty, glowing orange-hot and hissing steam.

The vines around the stone table had exploded into thousands of shreds of wood. Loesie sat on the table, looking around with a deep frown on her face.

The duke sank back against the cart, panting. "I let it escape." He balled his fist at the overhanging trees where a burnt hole in the canopy indicated the place where the demon had burst to freedom. "I let it escape!"

Johanna had no idea why he had thought that he could capture a magical being in a tiny iron cage, but she was glad that it had gone and that the duke could not harm anyone with it.

"Johanna? What we be doing here?" *That* was Loesie's voice. She rushed to her friend and closed her arms around her shoulders. Loesie felt cold and frail. The hand that reached up to Johanna's arm trembled. Her fingers were so thin and bony, her lips cracked and bleeding.

"Did the fire hurt you?"

"I din' see no fire. What sort of place is this? How'd we get here?"

"It's a long, long story. We better go back to the house. Are you hungry?"

"I could eat a horse."

At that moment, Sylvan just came out of one of the tree tunnels leading the horse and wagon. "See, there be a horse. Someone's listening to me." She laughed.

That was the old Loesie.

"Is she all right?" Sylvan asked.

The duke said, "She is very strong. I don't know who did what to her, but it must have been a strong magician. I think we got most of the spell, but there may be a lingering effect. She'll have to come back here if that is the case."

Loesie frowned at Johanna. "Why do these people talk funny? What's this with spells and magicians? I thought ye city folk din' believe in magic."

"We're a long way from the city." Johanna helped Loesie off the stone table. She might have been cured, but her muscles were very weak. She leaned on Johanna's shoulder and was breathing heavily by the time they reached the cart.

"I be no magician, Johanna. Tell them that. I want not a thing to do with magic anymore. It's evil."

Johanna agreed with her, but the problem was that magic would happen no matter how people denied or forbade it. She climbed in the wagon and sat next to Loesie on the back seat. Sylvan helped the duke in before leading the horse through the tree tunnel back up the hill.

Karl waited at the end of the tunnel with Sylvan's horse. He climbed in the driver's seat while Sylvan mounted his horse. He looked tired, too.

He stared over the meadow and into the blue sky. "Did you see where this thing went, Karl?"

"All I saw was a sudden ball of fire that leapt in the air. It went higher than I could see, and then it was gone. Nothing I could do."

The duke shook his head. "I didn't expect you to do anything. It's all right, even if it's a pity that I couldn't catch it."

The horses broke into a slow trot down the hill. Loesie leaned against Johanna. Her head rested on Johanna's shoulder and grew heavy and warm.

No one said anything on the way back, but the bird song seemed more cheerful and the sunlight brighter than before. When they arrived at the house, Karl helped get Loesie down from the wagon. She woke up enough to support her own weight, but that was about all. Considering how long it had been since Loesie had slept properly, she had a lot to catch up on.

The duke said. "She will probably sleep most of the day. Longer, if she has been under this spell for a while." He rubbed his face. "I'll probably sleep for a while, too."

Sylvan helped Johanna take Loesie up the stairs to the front door. She could see Nellie's face behind the upstairs window.

They entered through the front door into the cavernous hall that had dispelled most of its eeriness and had become plain stuffy.

"You'll have to forgive my father," Sylvan said when they were slowly walking up the stairs. "He hasn't done any of this for a long time. We don't see many people who are this badly affected by magic."

Did they see many people here at all? "I've . . . never seen anything like this. Is fire magic common?" She wanted to keep him talking. As yet, this place raised far more questions than answers.

"Not common at all."

"That is an extremely powerful type of magic." *Powerful enough to burn an entire city.*

"It's not the most powerful. Destructive, yes, but not

easily controlled and not hugely useful in everyday life. Do you know that you can always tell a fire magician by the creature his apparitions take on? It's the only type of magician you can identify from their magic signature."

Was he trying to tell her in a roundabout way that the duke hadn't been in Saardam? Was it even true what he told her? "Do you know anyone whose fire demons look like giant cats?"

Sylvan turned to her. "Leopards? With spots?"

"I don't know. I wasn't close enough to see spots. Do you know who that could have been?"

"Cats are common as fire creature. I would really need to know if there were spots to tell who it was. Where did you see this?"

"Fire demons caused the burning of Saardam."

He gave her a sharp look. "My father has nothing to do with that, before you ask."

"According to what you've just told me, I gathered as much." *If it's the truth.* "That's why I'm asking about large cats. Can you give me some names of possible people?"

"I am not allowed to, unless I have evidence to clearly identify the person."

"Allowed? Who doesn't allow you to give names?"

"The magician's guild. They control the practices we adhere to. There is enough rumour and untruth circulated about magic without us adding to it."

"A magician's guild?"

"They're normally fairly quiet and don't draw attention to themselves. It is a place of knowledge and academia, where people learn about magic. I recommend that when your friend is ready to travel, you go on to Florisheim to seek out the guild. You will need any knowledge you can get." His eyes met hers in a penetrating way that made her certain that he knew who she was, he knew who Roald was, and he had known this all along.

And it would be really nice if she understood why the duke had sent men to get them off the *Lady Sara* before it reached Florisheim. Surely *Giving weary travellers a bed* was not the reason.

CHAPTER 14

THEY CARRIED Loesie into the bedroom. Nellie opened the door and folded back the covers. "Oh, that dress is disgusting. We should really do some washing, Mistress Johanna."

"Let me know what you want washed and I'll ask Gertrude to take care of it," Sylvan said.

Gertrude, presumably, was the dour-faced servant.

Johanna sank down on the edge of the bed when Sylvan had left. After all the excitement of the morning, she felt really tired, too.

She straightened the blankets over her friend. Loesie was asleep, on her side, with her knees drawn up and her hand curled up into a relaxed fist and pressed against her cheek. She looked peaceful, like a child.

Nellie watched from the other side of the room, as if still afraid to come close. "Is she going to be all right?"

"Maybe." Johanna wasn't sure that Loesie was entirely cured yet, and wouldn't believe it until she had spoken with Loesie and knew that she remembered everything that had happened to her on the farm. "It will be a few days until we know for sure, but it looks promising."

She remembered the vines growing over Loesie and the fireball bursting from them. All those things seemed to be such a long time ago already, as if they had happened in a different time and different place.

"Where is Roald?"

"Oh, my excuses, Mistress Johanna. I discovered that the duke has a really amazing library and I showed him. I've been unable to get him to come out, even to see you."

"That's all right. I'll go and see him later."

"He never even asked about you."

"That's fine. It's the way he is. No one can change that."

Johanna went to her own room and tried to sleep, but there was too much to mull over in her mind.

The most important thing: the duke and his son had been unfailingly kind and helpful. And yet she couldn't shake the feeling that they were somehow lying to her or trying to lead her—and Roald—into a trap. She worried that they were walking into this trap with their eyes open, or had already done so. But if they had, she couldn't see it.

After a while lying on the bed staring at the ceiling, she got up and went downstairs in search of the library.

It was eerily quiet in the house. Her footsteps echoed in this horrible dark hall. Even the servants seemed to have disappeared. The paintings of the duke's ancestors on the wall were so lifelike that in the dim light, Johanna sometimes thought that the people in the paintings moved. She stopped several times to read the notes engraved in small plaques in the frame, giving the painter's name and the name of the person who had commissioned the work.

The duke's grandfather had been a tall man, like Sylvan, with penetrating blue eyes. Johanna could almost feel the magic radiating from the painting.

She found the library at the end of the downstairs hallway where the dining room was. It was a high-ceilinged room with the walls covered in bookshelves. Because the ceiling was so high, a wooden gallery ran along the walls to have access to the top shelves. Father had a couple of shelves of books, beautifully written, with coloured plates and bound in gold-embossed leather. Some of them, such as Rinius' *On the Movement of Stars*, had been Father's presents to her. To have as many books as they had at home was considered a treasure. She could barely comprehend what this library must be worth.

Roald stood in the very corner of the gallery, reading a thick book. He didn't seem to have heard her, so Johanna padded up the wooden stairs, sliding her hand over the railing. The wood showed her the tranquillity of the room. The duke seated by the fire, reading. Sylvan copying diagrams. Gertrude dusting the shelves.

"What are you reading?"

Roald gasped and looked over his shoulder. He turned around. The book in his hands was a copy of *The Anatomy of Man* and he had it open on a page with the title *The Woman With Child*. It displayed a drawing of a woman's body with a swollen stomach, cut open to show a child inside.

Roald's eyes met hers. Another man would have looked guilty, but he simply eyed her stomach, which was distinctly flat.

"That's what's going to happen, right?"

"Um, yes."

He continued to stare, first at the book and then at her, as if comparing the two. "It says here, 'The woman should not exert herself, should not expose herself to the elements, or ride a horse.' You should be careful."

"Later, yes." When it became obvious that she was with child.

Johanna stared at the page, but succeeded only in making herself feel sick at the sight of the woman's cut-open stomach.

Being married meant bearing children. It wasn't just about having no fun. It was about the ordeal and the pain and the fact that many women didn't survive. Her own mother had died while with child, although not in childbed. How could she tell if she was with child? Not for a while yet, that was for sure. Way back in Saardam, so long ago that it seemed another century, Augustina talked about quickening. Johanna had been disgraceful enough not to show any interest. She didn't want babies, right?

She was saved from an uncomfortable discussion when the door to the library opened and two people came in. One she recognised immediately as Sylvan.

The other was Kylian.

He looked up at the gallery, turned to Sylvan and nodded.

There was no longer any question about their identity.

"I'd like you to meet my cousin. He is a physician and he insisted on seeing the young lady afflicted by magic."

"She is asleep."

"So I heard from the other young lady." His eyes met Johanna's with renewed curiosity.

Johanna made sure that she went down the stairs first, to protect Roald. Now that her and Roald's identities were in the open, she felt strangely relieved. That was one thing she no longer needed to worry about.

She met Kylian's brown eyes.

He gave a small bow. "Fancy meeting you again here."

Funny, that, seeing as the last time she had seen him, he'd vaulted the fence at the palace, just before it burned.

"One could say the same about you." Haughty, detached. Yes, maybe she could do this royal thing.

"The duke is my uncle. I regularly use his estate as a way house."

"So I've heard." *Do you know of the dead bodies?* "You spoke to my maid this morning. Why didn't you come into the house for breakfast? You could have met us all there."

"I had my own matters to attend to. I presume you saw the farm on the way to the crossing point? I run those farms for my uncle. I arrived very late last night. My uncle told me of the possessed girl he had as guest. He said he was going to attempt an exorcism and asked me if I would like to have a look at her when it was done." Then he saw Roald. "Oh." He laughed and bowed. "Your Highness." He bowed to Johanna, too. "To you, too. I heard about your interesting marriage."

So much for Nellie not telling him anything.

"When your friend recovers, you must come with me to Florisheim where we can have a proper ceremony. My father will be most happy to host it, as he is already hosting many of your citizens. Several had told me that they had seen the heir to the throne escape the palace—one man even helped him— but he had not turned up at Florisheim with the others. So when I heard the rumours of a halfwit man with three women travelling upriver, I guessed it was you."

Sylvan gave him a cold look.

"Let us go and see this friend of yours."

"She is fine. She was very tired when we came back and she is resting now."

"I only need to see her briefly. I can feel if she has any residual magic in her."

There was no dissuading him from seeing Loesie, and to be honest, she wasn't quite sure why she didn't want him to see her, so they went up the stairs. Sylvan again came with them. She met his eyes while walking up the stairs. His eyes were penetrating. Johanna had no idea what he was trying to tell her.

Upstairs in the corridor, the sunlight came in through the window at the far end.

Nellie sat by the window sewing the holes in Loesie's old dress and rose as soon as they came in. "Kylian." She curtsied for him, with a very strange expression on her face.

Kylian gave her a cursory glance and sat on the edge of Loesie's bed. He reached out for Loesie's cheek.

As soon as his fingertips touched the skin, Loesie's eyes flew open. She inhaled a sharp breath and held it. Her eyes widened.

A chill breeze went through the room.

Kylian laughed. "You can't harm me with magic, little sorceress."

Loesie fell back into the pillow, looking dazed in a *why did you wake me up?* kind of way.

Kylian bent closer. "Do you remember who did this to you?"

Loesie frowned. There was no lingering magic now.

"Do you remember someone casting a spell?"

Her frown deepened.

For a long time, Loesie said nothing. Johanna only heard the thudding of her heart.

"Well," Kylian said eventually. "I'm sure the memory will come back." He rose. "She'll be ready to travel within two days. I'll accompany you to Florisheim."

He rose again and left the room. Sylvan ran after him.

After he had shut the door, Nellie smiled at Johanna. "Isn't he absolutely handsome?"

Loesie said, "He be a strong magician. No good fer church girls."

"Any better for farm girls?"

"I weren't saying that. I were saying that he'd be looking fer a noble girl."

"What's this about?" Johanna looked from one to the

other. Nellie, studiously pushing the needle in and out of the fabric of her dress, and Loesie with her arms crossed over her chest.

"Nothing," Nellie said.

Loesie snorted. "Ye want that man fer yesself. That's why."

"I don't," Nellie said, a bit too abruptly. "And if you're going to come with us, can you at least learn to speak properly?"

"I'll learn no townsfolk talk."

They glared at each other. Nellie stuck her chin in the air.

"Be nice," Roald said. "My mother says we all need to be nice to each other."

Loesie snorted. "Well, that be tough luck, because life isn't nice."

"Don't speak like that to the prince."

Loesie frowned at Roald. "The prince?"

"Prince Roald," Nellie said in a prim voice. "That will be 'Your Highness' to you. Same as Mistress Johanna. She's married to him now. Show some manners and respect."

Loesie frowned at Johanna. "You're kidding, right?"

Johanna shook her head.

"Holy cows. I missed the party."

CHAPTER 15

TALKATIVE AS LOESIE had suddenly become, she did not seem to have any recollection of how she had ended up mute, no matter how Johanna asked.

Johanna asked her about the demons which the basket had shown her, and Loesie just gave her a blank look. She asked about Loesie's family but the mention of them didn't seem to evoke any emotion from Loesie.

Kylian had declared her *fit to travel*, but what had really passed between him and Loesie?

There were more questions than answers.

The nice weather held for the next couple of days. Roald insisted on spending most of that time in the garden. There were wilted flowers on the roses, he said, and he simply could not tolerate that. Johanna wandered around the gardens and the lake, looking at the swans and the duke's ducks and peaceful sight of Roald pottering in the rose beds.

Loesie came outside on the third day. Even in three days, she had gained in health. Her skin was no longer ghostly white and her hollow cheeks were starting to fill out. During each meal, the duke urged her to eat more.

Johanna still didn't have a satisfactory answer to the question of whether he was more than a friendly old man who happened to have powerful magic. She spent some time in his library trying to find books about magic, but there weren't many, and those he had covered things like recipes for potions. Magic books, he said, were extremely rare, since most magic lore was never written down for fear of persecution.

The only one who still seemed tense was Sylvan. The duke laughed when she mentioned this to him, and said that Sylvan was never at ease when sleeping in a house. His son's bedroom, the duke said, mostly went unused because Sylvan slept in the stables with his bears. He said Sylvan was greatly disturbed by his bear magic because it could so easily be used for evil.

Johanna tried very hard to believe that these were good people, but could not dispel her unease completely. They might be perfectly friendly mass murderers.

She was glad when, on the fourth day, Kylian brought a coach to the front of the house. They packed up their meagre possessions, bolstered by some clothing which the duke insisted they take with them.

The most welcome bit of news was that Kylian said his men had brought the *Lady Sara* into Florisheim. The sea cows, he said, were all fine.

The duke and Sylvan insisted on coming with them on the ride to Florisheim which, Johanna gathered, was much closer than she had thought.

They rode out over the estate's main lane. Johanna sat next to Roald near the window. The duke had insisted that they dress well and take those visible positions in the coach, because *there might be some fuss*. Refugees from Saarland had learned that their prince had survived.

The duke had also lent Johanna some of his wife's jewellery, because *you simply cannot face your citizens wearing a farm dress*. That had really hit home to her that from now on, nothing in her life would be either a secret or the same.

Before getting on the coach, Johanna had stood in front of the mirror in the bedroom saying to her reflection, "You're a princess now."

She agreed she didn't look like one. So, she needed jewellery. Heavy gold pieces with glittering stones. She had insisted that she would return them to the duke as soon as she could, but he just waved his hand and said something about rather seeing the pieces being worn than stowed away in some wardrobe.

So here she was, dressed up like a slightly old-fashioned noble woman, facing Nellie, who was dressed up like a slightly less noble woman and sitting next to Roald, who looked distinctly uncomfortable in his stiff nobleman's clothes. The duke sat next to Nellie, explaining about all the places they passed. The estate's farms and what he grew there, the wineries, the creeks, the water mill, the estate's boundary and the village.

Sylvan sat on Johanna's other side, dressed in black and staring out the window with a brooding expression on his face. Loesie sat opposite him, making faces at him, to which he reacted by looking angrier.

They hadn't been travelling for long when the coach rounded a bend in the road and Florisheim spread before them. The town lay on a slight slope, a mass of terracotta roofs and stone that covered the undulating land on the left bank of the Rede River, whose mirror-like surface reflected the town.

The castle stood at the highest point, a grey stone

building with two forbidding round towers and a high wall, overlooking the town like a protective mother duck.

The curved line of the quay hosted a good number of barges. Low, flat, *Saarlander* barges, many flying the flag of Saardam.

Johanna's heart beat faster.

Father.

What she wanted more than anything was to check on the *Lady Sara* because surely if Father was here, that's where he would stay.

The duke told her that the baron had allowed the refugees to camp in a piece of land close to the river, a bright green meadow on which stood a collection of mismatched tents. A couple of boys in typical Saarlander trousers played sword-fights with sticks between the tents. A couple of women stood talking to each other, their long and wide skirts achingly familiar. Johanna even spotted a couple wearing clogs.

As the coach entered the grounds, people stopped their activities to watch. They called other people, who came to the tent entrances.

The coach came to a halt in the middle of the camp. By now, a veritable crowd of refugees had gathered. The wobbling of the coach signalled the driver getting down and coming to open the door.

"Look, look! It's prince Roald!" someone shouted.

Johanna's heart beat faster. Roald sat with his hands clamped between his knees.

"Let me go first," she whispered to him.

He didn't react, but she put her hand on his. His skin felt clammy with sweat. He swayed from side to side ever so slightly.

"Shhh, calm down. You don't have to speak. I can do that." She fished the chain with the ring from under her dress, undid the clasp and slipped the ring on her finger. Her hands, too, were trembling. What would people say about this?

The door opened. The driver reached in. "Your Highness."

Roald went first.

A great cheer went up outside. Holding onto Roald's arm, Johanna could feel him tense up.

"Prince Roald is alive!"

"Three cheers for the new king."

He had frozen completely, still on the coach steps.

She whispered to him, "Roald, take one step down, then I can come out, too. I will talk to them." *Please don't start swaying or banging your head into something.*

The muscles in his arms were so tense that she could feel their hardness through his jacket.

"Roald, please?"

She pushed him gently, and he took a stiff step to the ground.

People cheered and clapped.

"Three cheers for the new king!"

"We are saved!"

But Roald stood there frozen, his face a mask of terror. Any moment now and he would start screaming, or rolling on the ground, or laughing like an idiot.

She pushed past him, waving her hands. "Give him some room! Please, people."

Then their attention turned to her.

"Why, it's Johanna Brouwer."

And then a woman said, "Is that the Carmine crest she's wearing?"

A voice behind them called out, "Make way for their royal highnesses, the prince and princess of Saarland." It was Kylian, standing on the driver's seat of the coach.

The people retreated and formed a path. Johanna held onto Roald's arm.

"Just keep walking," she whispered to him, while guiding him. "Stay calm. Keep walking."

In the crowd, she met the eyes of Julianna Nieland, in simple, dirty clothing, with hollow cheeks. She came forward and dipped a curtsy to Roald. And another to Johanna.

"Please, Julianna."

Julianna looked up with tear-filled eyes. "Is my brother with you?"

"No. Have you seen my father?"

A look of mutual pain went between them.

Then another familiar face met her in the mayhem. "Master Deim!"

The merchant wrestled through the crowd. He gave her a big hug. "Oh, child, I didn't think I would see your happy face again!"

"Where is Father?"

"He was upset that the *Lady Sara* was gone. He took the *Lady Davida* and that was the last I've seen of him."

"He's not here?" A black hole opened inside her. Father, dead?

Master Deim shook his head. "So many people are gone. The king and queen, the mayor, Reverend Romulus—"

"The reverend? Was he killed?" The thought made her sick. Who would kill a priest? "Is it true that Saardam is in the hands of a religious brother called Alexandre?"

"We've heard people say that, yes. We don't know how much of it is true."

A nobleman on Johanna's other side was speaking to Roald. "Your Highness, you must come with us. We must decide our next steps." He met Johanna's eyes. "Um, Lady, I'm unsure what the baron's son meant when he said . . . are you . . ."

"Married before the eyes of the Triune," Nellie said, behind Johanna. Dear old Nellie and her appropriateness.

The man swallowed. "Well. We, um, must . . . make it official."

He didn't like it, not at all.

The procession came to the edge of the field, separated from the riverbank by a road. At the jetty on the other side a welcome sight greeted Johanna. The *Lady Sara* lay amongst a couple of barges, most of them Saarlander, but one was a local ship with a large cabin, similar in build to the Burovian ship that had brought Roald to Saardam.

The duke said, "The baron provides you with one of his ships to use as accommodation. I guess this is where we say goodbye."

"Thank you so much for helping us," Johanna said.

The duke took her hand in a weak, paper-skinned grip. "It is nothing, child. One day, when you're settled back into your home town, think of us and do my son a favour."

Johanna met Sylvan's eyes. The look in his eyes alone was enough to stab someone through the heart.

The driver was already helping the duke back to the coach, but Sylvan stayed behind.

He leaned close, giving Johanna a much closer view of his tattoos and that horrible scar, far closer than she had ever desired. His expression was just as humourless and morose as before. "Look, I need to tell you something. I know you don't trust us. Given all that has happened, I can't blame you. It's probably a good thing. You are going to need all the wits you have to get through this and survive."

Kylian sat in the driver's seat of the coach, looking directly at the pair of them.

"My father and I survive in the same way. We keep standing in the face of daily betrayal, evil and worse. I'm not telling you to trust us, but I hope that our actions will speak for us instead. I hope that you at least trust us enough to believe what I'm going to tell you now. It's about my cousin, Kylian. Don't ever trust anything he says. As heir to the throne, he takes betrayal and reigning by terror to a new level. Once he has you in his sights, he does all he can to get whatever he wants. For the men, that is usually money or power. He will find something that you have done wrong in the past, and threaten to make it public. Then he'll come to you at all hours and act like he's at home. He'll demand favours—"

"Like an ice cellar full of dead bodies?" Johanna had said it before she could stop herself.

Sylvan gave her a blank look. "Like—what?"

"Discover something his victim has done wrong in the past, like an ice cellar full of dead bodies."

The look of total puzzlement on his face was very convincing. "I have *no* idea what you're talking about."

Johanna was by now shaking so much that she had trouble speaking. "On your father's land, not very far from where you recaptured me after we ran from the village in the sand, there is an ice cellar."

"Yes?" He frowned. "I think there might be. It used to be used by my uncle who owned that land before it turned into a useless desert."

"Go there, and have a look inside. Remind yourself what's in there."

"Whoa, why do you think we—"

"You're right. We don't trust you." She pulled off the heavy brooch and golden chain she wore around her neck and dumped them in Sylvan's hands. "Here. I'd take off the dress, too, if I had anything else to wear."

"But hang on. You turn against us after we've helped your friend get rid of—"

"Your father did that for his own aim. We were brought to

you as prisoners. Somehow along the way, you found out who we were and became all friendly. We don't need you, Sylvan."

She started to turn around to catch up with Roald and the others who had proceeded onto the jetty, but he grabbed her arm. "Listen to me. All right, distrust us. Believe whatever you want, but listen to this one bit of advice: please seek out the magician's guild before Kylian can take you there. We need to stay strong against him. There is one thing, one very important magical thing you should know about him." He fixed her with his grey eyes.

"And that is?"

"He's the most powerful dark magician you are likely to come across in your life. He's a necromancer."

Then he let go of her arm, climbed into the coach and was gone, leaving Johanna to stand reeling amongst the adoring citizens. The breeze that touched her skin seemed colder than the coldest of midwinter.

THANK YOU

For reading Willow Witch. The story continues with The Idiot King, where Johanna finds out what the locals are up to.

BOOKS BY PATTY JANSEN

www.ingramcontent.com/pod-product-compliance
Lightning Source LLC
Chambersburg PA
CBHW030630190726
48286CB00008B/2461